TURN
LEFT
OR BE
KILLED

NANCY ASHBAUGH

TURN
LEFT

OR BE KILLED

THE VANGUARD PRESS, INC. NEW YORK

Manufactured in the United States of America by
H. Wolff Book Manufacturing Company, New York.

Library of Congress Catalogue Card Number: 77–155662
SBN 8149–0692–3

Designer: Ernst Reichl

To James Henle

PART ONE

1
Friday, August 13. 8:00 A.M.

This is the last morning Fiona will listen to George making his snorting and blowing noises in the shower. She sips coffee in the sitting room. George is served his coffee in bed: something wives fail to supply, for which lapse Fiona is grateful. It is one of the reasons George has been paying her bills almost a year, and Walt the same before him, and tonight someone else.

Tomorrow is Saturday again, husbands' and wives' family-fun and wick-dip night; a lovely night for Fiona, because even a new man, her kind, a married man, won't come to see her.

George wants sex upon waking in the morning, after a restful sleep during what's left to him of the night following his torrid final bout upon arrival at midnight. At seven this morning Fiona slips from bed to use a vinegar douche

8

in case the foam has failed to live up to its claims; then she makes the coffee, serves George, and then herself.

She lights a cigarette, considering the dangerous pill. It may be lethal in other ways. Who knows what side effects can bring her to the attention of hospital authorities who will require name, address, and answers to prying questions and all that? The pill is not for professionals who look no further for more problems.

Fiona takes a drink and wishes George would finish, pack up, and leave. She will dream awhile into her picture on the television set. It may look a lonely scene to some, this image of quiet country farmyard appearing in the unlighted set, but not so to Fiona. In reality it is only an illusion, of course, created by a trick of the light reflecting sky and greenery from outside the front window that looks over the wild garden.

Still I do not complain, she tells herself, because it is very accommodating of George to announce his departure on this Friday morning of a very hot August 13, so I can go promptly to the Mar Vista this evening without waste of a single day.

The Mar Vista is a smart, beach-front hotel with primitive-island décor where corporation executives meet one another for an informal gathering they call their "Thank God, It's Friday" club. There, without loss of pay, she can begin on her next assignment, the new man.

Does George's wife know? About Fiona, that is? If so, how has she found out? But why else the shambling man of last Saturday? If true, what can Fiona do about it? She doesn't care, because it's the finish of George here, for whatever reason.

The shower is turned off. Good. He's shaving. She knows

his ex-army-officer routine, still a part of him even twenty years later. He's only a member of the National Guard now, but he keeps right on with his militaristic morning ritual. George is precise.

She lights another cigarette and stares into the blank screen with its shadowy image of the permanent lovely place. She can see herself in a fat-cushioned chair, rocking on a front porch, gazing at a garden draped with blooming lilac and scented honeysuckle. The leaves twist and writhe dramatically, fanned by a slight breeze. The sky in the glass of the screen is clear blue and unsullied by strung electric wires and poles. Most of all, with George scraping away at his beard, there is sterile quiet within—not even screaming sounds of boulevard traffic from outside down the block. There is nothing to do with a city in this lovely scene she leans toward. It is a peaceful, beautiful picture, a vision of utopia reflecting back at her from the mirage on the un-lighted screen of the dusky quiet set. Someday she will step into this place and never leave its tranquil solitude. She will live there to the last.

George is pulling his suitcase from the closet. The case has been crowding her dresses for almost a year. Good. She turns on the set. It responds with much snapping and crackling, as though catching fire or snarling in protest at being forced to come to life. The TV man says living in southern California affects some sets this way, but he doesn't think they ever blow up. . . . The vision of beauty fades, then vanishes altogether. It is replaced by the hearty Toby Mug face of the news announcer, who appears out of his mind with wet-mouthed excitement. Fiona can see he is having difficulty controlling his saliva as he usually does when he has something violent to report. A murder, for example, with action shots of the body being carried out shrouded in canvas and bound with stout buckles and belts. His lips gleam brightly as his face gives way—mouth still working rapidly in staccato speech—to a scene on a hillside dotted with scrubby brush, all of it dry, hot, and parched in August. In only a moment she sees what the man with his nervous delivery is electrified about.

A small animal pants along, exerting every bit of strength to run at top speed up the side of a tall hill, so steep as to be almost perpendicular. Tiny, frantic-like puffs of sand spurt behind its feet and its tongue hangs long and dangles as it searches upward through an area of sparse weeds and twig-high growth that offers it no sanctuary anywhere.

Fiona's heart beats rapidly as she watches the animal's nose-to-the-ground determination to move its body, a blur of color to match the hot sand, up the side of the hill. Fast drums beat loud in her ears and her gulps for breath are timed exactly with the struggle of this small creature—"a female wolf escaped from the park zoo," howls the Toby Mug. "Trouble with the remote cable," he adds to excuse the shouting.

The animal's lungs are convulsed and she reacts to the nick of the first bullet that strikes a paw. She holds it up in full stop as though in wonderment, head hanging low, tongue lolling from her jaws. Another bullet scores, this time the right shoulder. Blood trickles unbelievably glossy and vivid down the rocks. She slithers over them, crawling and trying to stanch the oozing flow with a quick lick at it. There can't be much pain, only numb shock, because she staggers ever upward, dragging the leg. The blood trails are an arresting sight because the bullets make such tiny neat entries. Evidently she does not hear the helicopter roaring overhead. She is deafened by the sound. The plane mutters, buzzes, and its great wings cast raking shadows about the dirt beneath its path and the rush of air stirs the top of the brush in a powerful downdraft.

Stalking policemen, guns held at ready, stumble upward, closing in for the kill. The animal is finished when the next gunshot strikes. Its body flinches, then tumbles helplessly onto its side; after a few twitches and shivers, it lies stone still. Cameras move in to pick up any final quiver from the shrunken-looking lump of dull gray fur with beige under-markings. Sunlight catches a glazed eye, open in death.

Officers in black and white, hulking tall, like giants, stand high over the small body and look down at it. They speak in spent, gulping breaths to the on-the-scene, eager newsman who takes over for the Toby Mug. Black boots nudge at the body. Fiona goes close to the set and stares at the animal. The Toby Mug pans in again to describe another exciting piece of news, the Watts riot; he slobbers about it, talking rapidly. He is imprisoned at the studio for this one, and can't even get a remote for the action shot into Watts because of the uprising. The citizens have fenced out the Toby Mug with fire, bullets, bricks, and stones. His camera truck was turned over and burned only last night. This is the second day of anarchy, says the Toby Mug, and Fiona turns the set off.

Poor George! He is hoping to be called up with his National Guard unit to help quell this revolt of the unsatisfied, taking-the-law-into-its-own-hands kind of citizens in southwest Los Angeles.

George often tells her of his strong yearning to go to war. He hopes to bury himself behind the lines again, he tells her, in that good old gang of horse-on-you and throw-the-

12

dice-in-the-leather-cup-again boys, in an officers' club some-place—one of those slapped together of straw and sticks, a Vietnam kind of wilderness where adorable native girls wander about in slit-up-the-sides, form-fitting gowns and, best of all, so small all over. Like most men, he likes them best small. He can pretend he is in bed with a nine-year-old, as most men she's known like to imagine. Some part of her own success lies in the fact she's small and that she even has dark hair and eyes like a native girl. Of course she's not new to George any more.

He is whistling and she can see the way he purses his lips and holds them puckered; a neat trick this is, folding these broad and wide sensual lips into a tight bouquet for whistling. He is happy with himself, his bright whistling tells her, and for the hope of the chance to squeeze into uniform and direct men to put down a riot. This one is almost war, the newscasters are saying. She can see the way George's curving smile grins at itself in the bathroom mirror, with his eyes all lighted up and eager. George is good. He pays in advance the rent on this hidden tomb of gray cement.

The house is surrounded by tropical plantings and ivy so thick, even across the front gate, it may not open any more for all she knows. The mailbox just inside is all but buried. But the mailman never opens the gate. He reaches across among the leaves to drop his occupant and fourth-class-mail offerings. Since the rent is paid a month in advance, she reminds herself, no landlord promptings will come to her in that box. Who writes to her otherwise? No one knows she is alive except her mother, who is not interested enough to write often. Fiona likes this area of sprawling Los Angeles. It is the almost-integrated beach area of Venice, only a short bus trip away from Santa Monica. Of course, her immediate neighborhood is an exclusive Caucasian ghetto except for a few Mexicans trying to sneak in. So far this race riot eddies right by her four-block area without anyone bothering to stop to fire the odd brick or two. . . .

Here is George.

"What are you planning to do?" he asks, suitcase in one hand and shaving kit in the other. He rubs the center of his back between his shoulder blades against the doorjamb. His suit of dark gray silk gleams in the faint light from the ivy-covered window. Oh, he can't wait to turn it in for the old army khaki.

"I shall be fine," says Fiona. "May even take a run up to see my mother." To herself she adds: Where my mother will feel inclined to call the police to clear me off the doorstep.

"Better shove. Got a lot of stuff going on at the office," says George, pushing himself away from the doorjamb. The telephone rings. "Yes," says Fiona.

"But I know he's there, so tell him," a voice bawls out in answer to Fiona's wrong-number ploy.

"All right," says George into the phone while his face turns ruddy. "Good. I hope they do call out the Guard. . . . She's nobody. . . ." And he claps the receiver onto the bridge of the phone with a sharp crack.

"Sorry about that; hoping to protect you; some kind of check going on at the office. Don't think I'm calling a halt to us because of her; forget it. Actually, defense contracts stepped up and someone is doing some checking; everyone checking everyone else, you know. . . . Let me know if there's anything I can do. You know where to reach me.

14

Glad you got your Chink sociologist; pretty sweet, huh, paid for yapping. He still coming, I take it," says George.

"He'll be here this afternoon. . . . Well, good-by George, good luck," says Fiona.

George puts the suitcase down and takes her in his arms. Pressing the shaving kit to her back, he kisses her several times about the face. "Well, better cut this short. I'm going to miss you—better believe it."

He snatches up the suitcase and treads firmly out through the kitchen to the back door, swinging one shoulder higher than the other in his usual cocky walk. "Bye," he calls over his shoulder and shuts the back door.

"Hasta la vista," says Fiona to herself, leaning against the white woodwork in the kitchen.

2
Friday, August 13. 9:00 A.M.

Fiona returns to the sitting room and looks into the dead television. She listens to the lock click on the gate of the back yard. The sound of a motor catches in the alley that is called the Court. Years ago an artful builder hoped to be piquant when laying out the area, and named the alleys behind the houses the Courts, and permitted only a narrow sidewalk before the houses to separate front gardens from each other, the sidewalks to be known as the Place. All cars and delivery vans use the Court and only the postman is ever seen to use the Place.

"Seconna Place in front, Seconna Court in back, Fiona Place and Court," Fiona says aloud.

George is gone. The sound of the car retreats down the Court. She stares through the ivy to the wild front garden.

"George is gone," she says aloud, and goes to the bedroom and picks up his pillow. Beneath it lies the last white envelop she will have from him. Tonight, out in the world again. She opens it. Five hundred dollars spill to the pillow; extra severance pay: enough for a second-class ticket across the sea. Or shall she stay here and try to save, and maybe the outside chance will come she can buy her scene on the dead television and turn it into the real thing instead of staring at make-believe?

Yes, it is a relief George is gone. He begins to complicate her life when the wife finds out Fiona exists, not to mention her telephone number. Next, this wife will ferret out the address if she has engaged a detective, and she'll be right over to slap Fiona's face or claw her eyes out. She cares little that the wife has such information if she can be counted on to keep it to herself or between themselves; but this woman, like all her kind, will wish to share it with those men of the law who enforce moral legislation with a right good will. Fiona will be revealed.

Once she is counted up by a census taker, recorded someplace as alive, she will be in a fearful position. Fiona works years to remain unknown in an age when this is all but impossible for most citizens. She can very well come to light

16

through the machinations of a revengeful wife. That will be too bad.

Can George be frightened? For a week he's been unlike the old, carefree, blustery George. George is subdued, he is almost broody; most disturbing. But George is safe since, unlike herself, these current snoopers in his office know he is supposed to exist. And he's had snoopers in his office before in a corporation where defense—or is it offense?—is the main business. Why is George all but fearful of his wife while pretending indifference? Why would his wife want to queer him at work, thus cutting off her own money supply? She would not; therefore it must be Fiona she is after.

Besides, Fiona knows if there is a suspicion of George to do with his job, it is a lie, because all George is interested in is "sexing it up," as he puts it, good food and booze, airplane trips about the world, and a chance to get into uniform and action. "Strike first" is George's motto.

She hopes they manage to get the National Guard called out for duty in Watts. He will be pleased. Right now the news says they are having some difficulty in pinning down the authority and permission for such a move and so make George happy in this way. All this is not my problem. I can waste no time on George and his troubles. . . .

Fiona opens the closet door and air allowed into the wardrobe makes the black nylon raincoat sway with a swishing sound. It has elegant deep cuffs studded with a dainty spray of tiny rhinestones. She smooths it and it whispers a rustling sound; the stones glint and gleam at her. It's the most dramatic article she owns, except it's a nuisance on dry days, which fortunately are not so many in southern California. But now the August heat prevails. She takes it off the hanger and slips her bare arms into the folds of it and feels a prickling warmth shoot through her. The silken hair along her arms rises from pores as though by eerie outside force. Her skin tingles inside the sleeves and along the back of her bare neck. Even when she removes the coat, the sensation continues and there is the actual sound of minute crackings and snappings, like the television set warming up.

She slips it on again and it clasps her and enfolds her and encircles her almost without any help from her hands. An iron maiden? A shroud? Hell. Fifty cents she's paid for it in a thrift shop, and the label says it has come from an expensive shop along the Miracle Mile. Someone has not been able to stand the uncanny sensation it provides. She peels it off and it is reluctant to part with her; it whispers mysteriously at her as she must press it back into the closet. She tucks the envelope of money into one of the deep patch pockets and it stirs as she touches it and billows out to her and must almost be scraped away from her bare arm.

She pulls on a pair of black pants, adds a black silk blouse, and over it a beige linen sleeveless tunic. She looks a royal-court page in doublet and hose. She picks up a bag of soiled linen, a box of soap and a bottle of bleach, and with the ostrich-skin handbag beneath her arm locks the back door and goes through the yard to the Court, where, as always, she is sickened by the smell of filth, garbage, and smog; appalled at the sight of spilling, overloaded cans and boxes along its edges not due to be emptied until tomorrow, Saturday. Now the sounds of the snarling traffic come loud from the boulevard, assaulting her ears, and the scrabbling tiny wolf doomed to death is suddenly pictured too vividly in her head. She quickly blots it from her mind and replaces it firmly with thoughts of Humel, the sociologist.

She will miss George. He is nice to have around; sheathe his sword in bed and he is quickly satisfied, and so neat and clean about himself too. One day he asks, "Fiona, why did you become a prostitute?"

"I guess I just got lucky," she tells him, and he laughs and tells her she's so witty.

In the profession one of the main things that attracts is this matter of hygiene; she must tell that to Humel, her Chinese sociologist, doing his investigation for a paper in his graduate study. All this money for her and no sex; required only to mouth along and for cash. Poor George! No wonder he is suspicious in the beginning when she tells him about Humel's request for her time.

George says he must be okay. Who but a nutty, harmless, perennial college man—on yet another thesis, for yet another degree, who, one and all, never make it to synthesis —will pay a prostitute just to listen to the sound of her voice?

Fiona is paid for past experience, she tells George happily, pointing out that in other words she is getting double pay. Pretty good, she tells George. He teases her, saying he can't believe any red-blooded man wants simply to listen to Fiona James yap, a high-status, chit-chattering whore, and he laughs . . . but not lately; this is weeks ago now.

Humel also seems interested in George. Maybe he'll be in the paper too—case history of a good customer. Humel asks many questions about George. A whore's gentlemen are an important part of a scientific study of prostitution, he says. Oh, there are hundreds of studies made of street-walkers, but none about girls of Fiona's stratum. Who pays her bills is of prime interest to a good sociologist making a thorough investigation. And the chance way she meets

Humel at the Mar Vista one night, while waiting for George to have dinner, is really a bit of luck. But, of course, she lets him know she's already taken. And when he asks for a series of interviews about her work—well, it simply floors her. She says yes.

Today she will serve him the paper-thin watercress sandwiches he likes and talk to him for another twenty-five dollars while she sips tea to keep her throat moist.

Stop distracting your alert attention with trivia and watch out. You're on the street in broad daylight and, in spite of smog, be careful, unobtrusive. Stay close to slanting garages, back sheds, and houses; keep your head down, walk briskly, Fiona admonishes herself. I am only another girl going to the washhouse with a black canvas bag of laundry in hand and looking too smart for being what and who I am. I should have worn jeans. She is passing the beaten-looking cleaner's back door, an establishment with a tall dirty mirror clinging to its wall and all-but-obliterated gold lettering telling of a brand of cigars long since gone, like time passed into oblivion. She glances at herself in the mirror, enjoying the distorted reflection in the wavering glass. It has weathered too many unfortunate days in the violent elements that make the weather picture of southern California, no matter the Chamber of Commerce brochures to the contrary.

She passes the old man's spy system, his yard given over to wires strung about. A rustling, booby-trapped electrical bell and warning system has been created so the old man can lie on his cot inside his backyard shack and hear anything moving outside his house, he tells Fiona one day with a leering, maddened glare. His toothless, while-sucking-at-his-mouth remarks remind her of Humel, the sociologist saying during one of their sessions, "Poverty begins in the teeth."

Ah, the boulevard! Doors begin to slam, people get into cars, out of cars, search for things in cars, speed by in cars —all the metal extensions of man hooting and honking at once and all the drivers giving one another filthy looks.

Now she is abreast of the painted pink house where the grocery man confides one day that an old woman has died and left to her no-good, lousy son a collection of forty hats by way of legacy.

A young girl goes by in red short shorts. Her blonde hair trails in long curtains to her waist, except for a tall pompadour cresting high over a low forehead. She looks at Fiona's overblouse, and checks her black pants and neat flat-heeled boots with measuring eye for detail and cost. Fiona looks away, still thinking of the dead old woman and the grocer who told her she also left a bullet-riddled car in her garage. "And the cops counted up sixteen bullet holes that someone had applied green paint to cover, but they could still be seen." So many of life's little stories have no rhyme, reason, sense, or even nonsense about them, simply asinine, and in the washhouse Fiona puts her clothes in, shoves twenty cents in the slot, and sits on a bench.

No blacks are present. Perhaps the riot has cleared them from the area. A woman plunks herself down next to Fiona. She has a pale face and looks like a weasel—even hairy, with fur on lip and chin. She confides, as though taking up the conversation from where she left off yesterday, with her chin hair in agitation, "Well, they've took my sister over to that Los Angeles college hospital and they sure did crap her up; sewed her up from outside in, instead

21

of inside out, and now her bladder is leaking all the time; tied her tubes. Wouldn't let them work on my pig in there."

Must be a damned bunch of people touched with genius, or how does one sew outside in? Fiona eases up and away to the bulletin board, where a man moves close enough to tell her how much he hates this dump because "You take the citizens around here, most of them make three hundred moves a month and leave no forwarding address. So who cares?"

God, she doesn't mind washing clothes; it's the people she meets. But at that it's one hundred percent better than the mess right here last week.

She removes her clothes from the machine, pushes them into the drier, sets it, and gazes through the dirty expanse of glass walling up the front of the washhouse that turns the people inside to roasting birds in a hot oven.

Once again she reminds herself that one little break and she can move on to another life. Ridiculous! What will you do with this break? What for? You come from nothing, you are going to nothing, so why bother to change things in between for nothing?

Still, if there is a chance, an opportunity to work at something, then she might not mind so much going to nothing. Hell. She folds the hot sheets and towels, packs them neatly into the bag, and walks the few blocks home. It is too hot to walk on to the Salvation Army. She will lay out her things for the hotel tonight.

Oh, they are at it again. She listens to them begin as she enters her back gate. The shrew who lives across the court screams at the old man they call Grandpaw, "Y'all stop lobbing them stones against this fence or I'm calling me the cops, you no-good bastard!"

"Listen, you son of a bitch," Grandpaw answers, shrilling it. "Y'all stop them dogs barking or I'm calling me the cops."

"Cool it, you old fool," says the shrew, and Grandpaw slams and bangs his wheelchair again and again at the fence, ramming it like a sheep. The woman crashes her back door closed. Four large dogs begin to bark. The little wolf—running, scrabbling, scrambling—flashes into Fiona's head; she is thinking about it again in spite of commanding herself to forget the damned wolf. Where will it get her, this brooding? Cheer up, look forward to getting out of the house tonight.

There is time now to straighten up the three-room house, make the sandwiches for tea for her guest, Humel, who pays and does not want her professional services. Every time she thinks of this she feels cheered. Of course, sooner or later she'll have to tell about her life at home and about her mother too, and she does not look forward to it. It is curious she's not been questioned along these lines before now. She does not care if he never gets around to it, but as long as he pays her he has the right to ask her anything he cares to.

She stacks neat sandwiches beneath a white napkin on a lovely plate edged in painted oranges. It is a plate she has found at the Salvation Army among crockery, glass, pots and pans, stacked and tossed into cardboard boxes up on the hot balcony. The day of this find she spends hours going through it all and has this plate by way of reward for filthy hands and tired back. So, unsuspecting and off guard as usual, she reaches up for the white earthenware teapot to place in readiness on the copper tray already covered with a stiff white napkin. She pauses to stare at its top, half on and half sticking up in the air. An earthquake while she is gone? Her fingers tremble. Not likely that without her noticing it only three blocks away. She removes the top and looks inside the pot. Nothing. She runs to the bedroom and examines the pocket of the raincoat and the money is there. She examines the room, turning slowly. Nothing. Back in the sitting room, she makes a complete survey. She can see nothing.

Yes, the crooked teapot top is extremely strange. She can't stand anything crooked, not even a picture on a wall, not to mention her lovely teapot, fifteen dollars' worth, that does not look lovely with its top half off.

Has Humel come early? He has no key. Humel will not unlock her door anyway and enter without her bidding. Humel is all politeness, gentle manners, and self-effacing. No, not Humel. The shambling man of last Saturday? But why?

Oh, God, the past week has been one unnerving incident after another! Now this. Well, finish up here: cups and saucers, tuck napkins of white linen, monogrammed with white embroidered J beneath sandwich plate. . . . The doorbell rings. Humel, of course. He is always prompt.

"How are you?" she greets him.

"I am well, and thank you," he says in his rasping voice. "May I come in, please?" he asks, stilted and formal as usual.

"Certainly. I have the tea ready. I'll be right with you," she says. She flicks the gas on beneath the teakettle, and leads him to the sitting room. He sits on the Lawson sofa she has found at the Good Will for ten dollars only three years ago.

It is a dirty gold with tiny green pine trees over it, but in fine condition, aside from its cover. So she has a velveteen slip cover tailored to fit it, made in one day of hard sewing, and now it glows with rust drama against the white painted wall. Orange satin and taffeta round pillows from Penney's are comfortable behind him as he leans back after placing his filled pipe deliberately on the edge of the coffee table of Vermont black stone. He fingers matches in his vest pocket. He takes no notes.

"How is George, then?" he asks.

"Fine, thank you." She does not intend to tell him that George has left, not yet; he may lose interest in her case history if she has no current boy friend supporting her. After tonight, when she has the new man, she will tell him.

She goes to the kitchen, pours boiling water over the tea leaves, and returns to the sitting room with the pot. She places the top on it precisely, willing herself not to think again of this odd development. But how can the strong, fat, wide lip of the pot suddenly climb up from its deep well and place itself tip-tilted on the edge of the teapot? It cannot be done without help. Whose?

"Fiona James is a nice name," says Humel, hissing the s's. "I like it. Do you know where your parents got it?"

"You mean Fiona, of course, because naturally James is not my name. I adopted it for the profession. I thought it had an elegant ring."

"No, no. Fiona, I am thinking of. That is your real name?"

"Oh, yes. I don't really like it, except it's different. In fact, I've never heard of anyone else with the name. Sometimes I dislike it a lot, since it reminds me of mammy slave names. 'Yes, mam,' in the kitchen to the madame, and she says, 'Fiona, we'll have soup today.' Fiona is like Willy May, Ruby, or Pearl."

"I see. . . . Do you know it is of Celtic origin? The meaning of Fiona is 'white'?"

"Having your little joke before we start to work I guess, because anyone, as soon as I was born, knew I was black, especially my mother. Ha, ha!" Fiona says.

3
Friday, August 13. 2:00 P.M.

Already Fiona is hoping Humel will hurry up, get on with it, finish up, and leave. Instead he looks cool, at ease, and all but grown to her sofa. In spite of attempts to control her mind, it continues to seethe with questions, beginning with the crooked teapot cover and ending with the shambling man of last Saturday.

She looks up from her folded hands in her lap to see a man walking slowly past the front of the house on the sidewalk. Someone walking along Seconna Place? His head hangs to his chest. No, he does not wear a brown suit, nor does he shamble briskly; he shuffles. Not the same man at all. Who is he? Not even a dog moves down the grown-over sidewalk between the houses, at least in daylight. Who can he be?

"I said"—Humel is obviously repeating, and for how many times?—"that, of course, one knows you are a Negro. I am asking how do you feel about this riot in Watts?"

God, she must pay attention. George is gone, but why invite Humel to take his money and leave as well? Foolish.

"What do you mean, how do I feel about it?" Fiona asks.

"Since you are Negro, do you feel sympathy or not in the resort to violence?"

"Not being in their situation, I don't think I'm qualified or entitled to pass judgment. I'm not under a table some-place, hoping for a crumb to fall my way. That's their situation, or so I've heard. At least some more candid than prudent have been suggesting it in the newspapers and on television. All I've seen for three days is riot news, and this is Friday."

"In your profession you say you are far from the main stream of the affluent society by choice."

"Let's hope so. I work at it. I don't even have a credit card. I don't exist. That's where these refugees from the South in Watts made their mistake. As soon as possible, after they were born, they should have sought cover. Still, that's not easy with the damned dark skin, I know. I had few choices myself."

"Most have some free will in many things," he says.

"Why don't you take notes during our ramblings? You must have an excellent memory," she says, to pay him out for his remark on free will.

"Yes, I have," he says.

Why do these quivering nerves prickle along her fingers,

27

curling out to grasp at the handle of her cup, so that for a moment she is fearful she may spill hot tea into the sandwiches?

"Were both your parents Negro, or part?"

"No. I was born to a white stepfather and from a white mother. I never saw my own father. Undoubtedly he was one-hundred-percent coal black. I was born into a place where, later, when old enough to look about, the only black I saw was a tiny old man who polished shoes in a barbershop in the largest hotel in town. You have noticed that my parents made me the original beige girl, a color once called tan. Say a room is done in beige tones, then I blend right into the drapes and rug, sort of a monochromatic walking color of many doctors' and dentists' offices. I also match currently fashionable wicker furnishings, like the trunk over there with the brass fittings I use to hold logs for this Franklin stove. Beige skin, small features, straight black hair sometimes help me pass, unless I meet one of the overt Klan types as I did in the washhouse this week, in which case I understand—or so it's said—'It takes one to know one.' "

"Have you ever had a Negro client?"

"No, always white."

Except the artist, a black who doesn't count; the last thing she asks him for is money. This man is none of Humel's business; not even her business now.

"George," Humel says. "How does he feel about the riot?"

"He is dying to help put it down. He hopes they figure out a way to get the National Guard called out. He adores war. This is the closest he can get to it at his age—about thirty-seven, I think."

"When does George come here? How often?"

28

"I guess your memory is not so good. I told you that last time. In fact, we've covered George quite well—his prowess in bed, always smiling, lots of strength."

Why doesn't Humel light that pipe? Always takes it out, puts it on the table. Maybe he has a bug in it; they can put them in an olive in a cocktail these days. Maybe his excellent memory is a lie. But why a bug? I really don't care in the least about his memory.

"George is in your life right now, so I am interested," he says.

Sometimes in these interrogations, when Humel is on George, he likes to feint, as boxers say about prize fighting, and come in with his fist from yet another angle. He seems terribly concerned with pumping me about George. She masks her eyes to hide the wary look, bends over the teapot, and carefully refills his cup. She selects a small sandwich and begins to munch, gazing at the dark screen of the television set. His face is bland, another mask. Who really wears a mask? She is the member of the masked profession. Why does he wear one? A person of his socially accepted attainments, and yet wearing a mask she can all but smell. She watches him covertly.

"For my study purpose of your profession, I am hoping for the timely, right-now, hot-off-your-griddle—as they say —kind of report."

She doesn't smile at his English. She listens and watches.

"I do not wish it to be static and slow. It will be good to permit me to follow you about for the next weeks."

"You sound like a reporter, or maybe a detective."

She feels about Humel today the way she does when she puts on the tingling black raincoat.

"Tell me . . ." he begins again, and she knows he will be

the sociologist now that he sees she is on guard. He will ease her. "About your family," Humel continues. She will give him his money's worth and keep him off George awhile.

"I don't know a lot about my family now. I don't go home. I am not presentable among white half sisters married to whites, who do not care to introduce black Aunt Fiona to their white children."

His black bead eyes, with the drooping skin folds at the inner corners, watch her hands. She folds them in her lap.

"Epts is my stepfather's name. He married my mother, I understand, before I was born. I don't know what my father's name was; perhaps Uncle Tom. I believe my real father was married before he met my mother. Anyway, it is all a very good thing when you think of it. Gave them all an out, all the way around, except for me, of course. One time my mother tried to tell me my real father was a Turk and a musician. Later she admitted he was black.

"You pointed out the whimsy of my name, Fiona. Once I saw a first name featured among high-class women—the right-race-and-creed women—in the society pages of the newspapers. The name was Whitney. I considered changing mine to Whitney, but then I decided to stay with Fiona and only change the last one to James. This was after I'd gotten a passport in my stepfather's name.

"On shipboard I met a girl from Turkey. She was dark-skinned, all right, even darker than I. Her eyes were black as olives; she had arching overhanging brows, and her nose reared out between them into a knobby beak and then went swooping down to a bowed tip, like a parrot's, over thick curving lips. I could see little resemblance between us. She had a strong face, tough, formidable. Mine is the

30

opposite; eyes, nose, and mouth assembled rapidly. The creator went quickly on to the next along the assembly line.

"I have a good figure though, and I'm terribly particular about my clothes; no fussed-up dress for me. I like the total tailored look. And everything fine too. I often buy men's linen handkerchiefs—very good ones, with hand-rolled hems—to make my underclothing and small blouses. I make them by hand with tiny stitches and use beige silk for my best things. When I make a white blouse, I use tiny buttons with a dull finish, never glazed or bright. My shoes are the best unadorned black kid, medium heels, never high. My stockings are black and sheer, and I never wear lace or faddish costume junk. My handbags are pin seal, ostrich, or pigskin, and gloves the best French or Italian leather I can find. For best I have a beige chiffon dress, very simple, round neck, not cut low, cap sleeves, beige shoes, and I wear one jewel—a topaz clip—at the waist. Mostly my entire wardrobe is black and tan. Black suit, tan scarf, et cetera, et cetera. I make almost everything. I pay twenty-five dollars for two yards of the best fabric to make a suit; I line it with silk."

Oh, she can see he is getting absolutely sick of listening to this yap. She goes on, "I make slipcovers too. All this furniture I bought secondhand. These shops are mostly for poor people and I lead a precarious life, so I am money conscious. That chair you sat in last time I bought for twenty dollars when George got to be a Colonel in the National Guard Reserve." (How his eyes light up like slot machines at mention of George!) "All the brown material I got for thirty-nine cents a yard at the import store to make the slipcover. I painted the walls white, front door to back.

I made the white chintz curtains and sewed small, thick, gold shag rugs together to make this big one in the center here. I covered the pillows with the same color gold for George's chair."

(His eyes gleam again at the mere mention of George!)

"You see, I am not dull. I have talents that would be especially fine to possess if I had a home, family, husband; and that is why I have these talents—the fates do not allow anyone to have everything. If, for example, I were a wife and mother, I would no doubt be only a fair cook and I would be helpless at sewing. I would need to hire someone to paint at four dollars an hour and I would require steady help for washing and waxing floors. I would have several large clothing accounts at the shops and there would be installment buying for furniture. I would need a car to get to all the shops and to corral the children while I shopped. Rather a pity things are so unfair. Not that I think wives feel badly about it. I am certain most of them know that the more they learn to do, the more they will be saddled with doing; and the less they learn, the less they'll be required to do."

(At long last I will permit him to say something and rest my throat. I am beginning to sound hoarse.)

"You believe your color has been the bar to your achieving in the more accepted manner?" he asks.

"That's it. My manners might be acceptable but not myself."

"Perhaps you make too much of the color business."

"Oh, I'm sure of that. Overly conscious, that's me. In fact, I've had skin color on the brain since I can remember. I used to think of my mother as the albino. She was the white, white, bleached color of worms to be found beneath stones when you turn them over; and she had blonde hair almost white, and pale blue eyes, and light pinkish eyelashes. Both my sisters were the same white, though my stepfather had black hair; but he had very light skin too.

"Take me, I would possibly be black as the ace of spades if not for my white-worm mother diluting my shade. As it is, I have come out the color of wicker and it is truly, terribly smart this season in furniture; all the house magazines are full of it. Let's say the ladies leave it out in the weather—wet wicker—then this is even more my color. Sometimes the paneling in the bar on a ship—say maple, oak, or even birch—are about my shade. I might be coming from the woodwork or be a part of some of the bars on which I've rested my elbow, a sort of lumped-up part, a wart the carver forgot to chip and smooth away. I am the color of a roast turkey, a lovely color dearly to be wished for in roasted turkey; or a chocolate cake lacking character, so that I did not turn out a deep brown with a red tinge to be found in good devil's food. Or I could match the top of a baked apple pie, first glazed with cream and sugar. Isn't it a shame I'm not furniture or food? Think how successful I'd be.

"Yes, I am color mad. I see my color everywhere: on grocery-store shelves, in five-and-tens, hotel lampshades, beige bedspreads, and thick rugs. If my mother had thought to make some stylized photographs of her children, she could have put her white daughters in black clothing, and her black daughter in white clothing, and won a prize in a black-and-white photo contest in the 'Saturday Review.'"

(The beads in his slanted slitty eye sockets are beginning to dilate and waver. Ah yes, they are. I'll pep him up with some sex talk.)

"I am lucky in some ways. In almost ten years in the business I've not had to answer phones like the average call girl. I've not been on the streets, of course; and never a part of the legal cow barns in Nevada, serving all comers by the grace of the state. I can count my clients on my fingers and I've even had long relationships. One time I had a friend almost two years before his wife, figuring she was getting on, thought she would be halfway decent to him, to insure at least his company for her remaining years."

"Do you find revenge in your work?"

(Ah, she's waked him up; his eyes are pointed flints!)

"I don't think so."

"For the color obsession, perhaps?"

"I don't know about the color business. I may have been responsible for a divorce, and one separation, and perhaps a case of rejection of one man by older children. But I've been hurt, if revenge may be canceled out this way, because an artist, a black, left me in London; in Rome he married a pure Milano girl with golden hair and blue eyes. A man in Paris left me; and in San Francisco, where I began, an Italian who had the lovely soft brown eyes of a deer, dropped me. I was madly in love with him. His militant mother brought up their church and engaged the help of priests and nuns and intrigued, pretending acceptance of the proposed marriage. She bought me extravagant and lovely clothes and she talked to another man, who would be the best man. When Bill was away at school, the best-man-to-be took me to dinner and appeared often at the flower shop where I worked—mostly in the back room, except when a black customer came in, in which case I was required to serve him.

"Bill's friend came in week after week, always with

candy, tickets to a show, something. He seduced me, of course; no problem, I couldn't resist such a large amount of professed love of me; I was not accustomed to so much attention lavished on me. Then the mother told Bill, and I never saw him again.

"The next man I met—thanks in part to all the lovely clothes Bill's mother had bought for me—took me abroad with him, and I went to the opera and ballet and theater and met the black artist, but that turned out no good. Then I met a rich American student and lived with him until he was finished with me. From there I returned to America and have been fortunate to meet top executives from large companies right here ever since. One man even wanted me to keep myself shaved down there."

"I see," says Humel, looking alive and shocked. (Hasn't got the stomach for it. And what a hypocrite he is! As though his country hasn't tossed unwanted female babies into rivers and bound the feet of those they kept to crippled stumps.)

"Oh yes," says Fiona, going on. "Stimulated him, felt more sexy, I guess. He could imagine I was a kid—hairless, innocent, young. Men like them young. It was hell, I recall, growing in again, needles and pins. Yes, we young, small, nicely shaded ones are prey in all the white men's countries. Take Vietnam; it's just more expensive back here.

"When my friends tire of me, I find someone else, and one man at one time gets all my attention. Perhaps I've been in need of that—arms about me, someone to touch with even the pretense of love. I paw at stray cats; pat kids on the head; yearn over flowers, trees; and admire old people. Maybe it's all those badges and decorations they've earned that are recorded on their faces and hands. I envy

35

them the guts they had to have to get them that far. If I'd married a white man, the children could have been black or maybe, worse yet, blotched. . . . No, I was not a victim of circumstance. Perhaps color, at first, but still, we seek our own level, the psychologists say. This one, no doubt, is mine."

4
Friday, August 13. 3:00 P.M.

"Aren't you in fear of strange men sometimes?" asks Humel.

"No, because I can put up or leave. Usually, a deviate turns out to have little more than a desire to fondle your feet. Funny, the way so many men simply like feet. Sometimes there's a request that you watch while he wanders past in various kinds of dress. My companions have been far from Corybantic; more staid, quiet, and close-mouthed, men of few words who like being entertained."

"And the law?"

"I'm extremely cautious. Anyone could turn me in; even neighbors could stir something up, anyone. But I don't sneak because of shame, since I'm not ashamed. I am discreet for self-protection. I don't feel degraded or dishonored. Perhaps one must feel noble or even appreciated to experience degradation. What is the difference between my being kept by a man and a girl with family brought to the board of trade at a ball and displayed like select meat in glittering plastic wrap at a counter for men to pick to marry? The girl often goes on marrying, too, until she's traded herself hopefully upward, moneywise, for the most she can manage."

"You liked boys as a youngster?"

"Yes, and I didn't mind women either. Now I rather dislike them. One time I thought of the religious stuff, entering a nunnery and all that, influenced by my mother, who had religion before she changed to fortune-telling. Now she makes lots of money at astrology."

"Is there a kind of man you prefer?"

Humel sits hunched over the coffee table, looking a shrunken dwarf of a man, but he's asking for answers, isn't he, with some claim to truth?

She says, "Oh, I think big men like George. Perhaps I feel more protected. And Bill was tall, the one responsible for my start on the ruined road, or I should say his hired friend, actually; he was a big man too. His actions made me think I was completely irresistible, and that he was out of his mind with my charms. Such flattery, such a build-up for me. And he swore he loved me. He gave me nice-tasting drinks, and caressed me and was very aggressive, but he had a lovely smile.

"Charm and determination at the same time is a good trick: Don't lose temper, always smile, gently touch, show much affection, and he 'makes out,' as the saying goes, and she hangs on to him.

"Most men, I've found, are charming and rather simple

37

as well. For instance, a man likes other men to see him with a lovely woman. He likes showing her off, and he thinks the more elegant she looks, the more other men admire him and believe him to be quite brilliant, or how else did he make it with such a wonderful girl?"

"Why do married men engage you?"

"Put off by their wives, and some are afraid of them. I don't have to be begged. Some men are rather sad at lovemaking, and in a minute it's over. To save his pride, I blame myself, but if I were his wife I'd teach him. Yes, I do feel sorry for men in some ways; they are quickly made happy. Love isn't involved; it's nothing to do with mind or spirit. Because I gratify an appetite it's no more corrupting than much else—perhaps, less."

"You can marry someday."

"These days men about my age get what they want free of charge from young girls, maybe cheap at first, but sometimes something else too, and that's expensive. In my trade I specialize in older men who open a wallet to show off wife and kids, and I know here's a man who will be interested in me. I could be a good wife—yes, I'd like to find a man who didn't know or, better yet, didn't care what I've done so far; he wouldn't have to have money, just want me. I'd even make a good mother, but I'll probably go on as I was born, alone, the way I've lived. Most love is rejected anyway; a person gets left with bits, except among wolves which, I'm told, mate for life, and no ring either. Isn't that odd? I mean about wolves being partners for life. . . .

"I don't expect a thing; in fact, I'd settle just for peace. You're condemned as a black in some places in this country even if your great-grandmother was only one-half black. It's like Hitler and Jews. So it may be difficult for me ever to find peace. There's Florida, where they make you a black if you've had a full black great-grandmother. Others say you are if you've got one-eighth black blood. It all comes out the same. Usually people decide about you by your appearance. About three-fourths of American blacks have white blood. In many places in this country it is against the law for me to marry a white man."

Fiona breathes slowly, winding down like a released, too-tightly wound-up clock. Humel's face is a shade warmer, more human.

"Perhaps you waste yourself. You are personable; you could go to the night schools, work at something by day. Many Negroes go to the night schools."

"I don't ask why you spend your life at sociology. It's all right with me," she says, watching his face cool off and stiffen.

"That is not the same; your work cannot be compared ——" And now his face is hard.

"I am paid to live with a man. Women who marry rich men are no different. If I'm a prostitute, what, then, are they? Everyone's a prostitute one way or another. In my case my mother thinks it's my fate according to the stars or something. I feel sorry for women, all women, even white women. There's always been unspoken contempt for them; two genders: men and sex. There's Shakespeare's seven ages of man, and there's a few stages for a woman too. In the beginning she's giggly and sly, then hysterical; next, crafty and marries the best she can; becomes emotional, and the menopause, and finally toothless, more or less as without significance as she began. She's born to be used and discarded. She's a vessel, a carrier; the insular contempt with which news announcers and journalists speak of all pack mules, ships, cars, planes as 'she'; even storms are given female names, and they never use the pronoun 'he' except when referring to a man. She's a breeder and mostly scorned later when she goes through the transformation of her gender, sex, to old woman. There is sympathy for men, boys, and starving kids, but not for middle-aged women. They yell 'women and children first' in a disaster, but that's because woman is a biological convenience and a necessity to continue the human race—of man, that is."

"You have compassion; you're not hard, in spite of the way you talk. I think you could be successful if you turn to something before too late."

"That's very good of you. I might have been a model had I been going on eighteen rather than twenty-five; at least I've noticed, as a result of civil-rights protests, perhaps, that dark-skinned models are sneaking into the Sunday 'New York Times' fashion ads and onto chewing-gum commercials on television; and into magazines like 'Harper's Bazaar,' where an entire issue was devoted to dark-skinned women, though the one I recall featured women of India. Still, their skins were black enough, or photographed that way."

"Then you could marry too," says Humel.

" 'Want you to meet the little woman,' my husband would say with indulgent disparagement. . . . Oh yes, perhaps, but so far I haven't met the man who wants to crusade, and I don't blame him."

"Were you rejected by your mother and, without a father of your own, did you, perhaps, become an outcast in your own mind?"

"On the contrary, I think my poor simple mother did everything she could think of with the rotten circumstance of having this black thing like a gleaming millstone slung about her neck for seventeen years. A mystery to me she didn't strangle me at birth. Instead she became a student of astrology, as I said, and she told me I am a Gemini and would have a marvelous life. She encouraged me to be fearless, and to leave home. She assured me I would be very lucky. Maybe she was right; it's not her fault my luck took this nonconforming turn."

The telephone shrills into the quiet. Fiona jumps. It has been still except for the sound of her steady mouthing.

"Oh, sorry," she says to Humel. "Yes," she says into the phone. "Yes, I see. . . . Not really. . . . Well, I won't be here tonight anyway. Not till late. . . . Don't worry. . . . Yes, he's here. 'Bye."

"Was that George?"

"Yes."

"I see."

(You would like to see more about George, wouldn't you? . . . Why?)

"George's wife is hysterical. She's bought a gun, but I won't be here. She can come if she likes."

(What's really on Humel's mind?)

"An unstable sort of politician on television the other night suggested all citizens buy a gun to protect their lives and property against the native uprising in Watts. He flourished his own by way of example and stated he was arming himself in the face of anarchy and the Watts insurrection. George just told me the Guard is called up and he gets to wear his uniform. George thinks that, in spite of his wife, I ought to stay home tonight and bolt doors and

41

call the police if anything happens around here. Some of the neighbors know I'm a black. Imagine me calling the police. George must be mad with excitement and out of his mind. And, Dr. Humel, you might as well know that George and I won't be seeing each other from now on. His wife, among other reasons. I never care to be involved when a man's family is stirred up; too dangerous for me."

"But this time I will appreciate it and for your good that you hang on with George," says Humel.

"Pardon?"

"See George as always. The people I am working for are interested in George."

"Oh, not really! Don't tell me you are one of these international spy types as well as a sociologist! If so, you are my first live encounter with the mad characters from all those conspiring stories."

"Just see more of George," he says flatly. "I will go now, but will see you the same time Monday."

"I do not care to see George."

"You don't wish to come to the attention of local or Federal law?"

"I will not be a spy of any kind; besides, I'm too nervous for it."

"That is too bad. You are already linked with one. The pipe is bugged; I have given you money in checks. The bug is not for my memory, it is for yours."

"You are wasting your time and money. George is no spy."

"It is not necessary. I am; and he can be used; we are good at it, and he wants to keep his job, and his wife upset too."

"Basically, I am fairly stupid. 'Sociology is the science that treats of the origin and history of human society and social phenomena, the progress of civilization and the laws controlling human intercourse.' I looked it up. Silly, wasn't it, because they left out spying."

"You are intelligent. So you can see there is nothing for you to do now except go along. George can use money and you can help."

She must let George know about this darling development. She must leave a note with the bartender at the Mar Vista this evening. She can't wait to get out of here anyway, with George's wife stirred up and prowling.

"What are you thinking?" asks Humel, moving now, as though he owns her house, through the sitting room to the kitchen and to the back door. She stands watching him and says nothing.

Humel reads her mind with ease. She is thinking she has met the shambling man's employer.

"The last Sunday you flew to Las Vegas with George, what did he do?"

"Nothing except gamble, swim, and eat. I earned my way in bed with him too, of course. And we came home the next day."

"This is odd, because I hear in Las Vegas you were sometimes alone. George has no interest in an explosion, for example?"

She will say nothing; give name, rank, and no serial number.

"I will see you Monday and maybe be in touch before. See George," and he opens the door and goes out. The latch on the back gate clicks behind him. A motor sounds.

She returns to sit on the sofa and to stare at the leafy delightful scene in the dark screen of the dead television.

It is difficult to find pleasure in this mirage of peace because intruding is the plain fact that if the shambling man of last Saturday is in the employ of Humel, who, then, is the man in Las Vegas?

The newscasters pronounce the name of Humel's big boss as Mousey Tongue. All the Humels ought to wear their identity so stupid people like Fiona can spot them on sight. Humel should wear tan, a drab, high-collared jacket and pants, a sort of uniform, with bright-red tabs by way of trim, and braid or something.

And George too ... what is he really? What's been wrong with George this past week? He isn't even so ape over sex. Most suspicious, because with George there is normally nothing else. Now that she thinks of it, she almost hates the faint memory of George. He is a swine who has got Fiona up a gum tree, proper, as the Cockney newspaper-vending old woman will say if Fiona confides in her tonight. She's her only friend. Maybe she can say hello to her tonight. What would it be like to have a friend indeed when one is in need?

Damn George and Humel and all their legion of friends!

Yet there is one thing. She's not seen the shambling man since last Saturday. That's something. Unless his first cousin walks down between the houses today while she talks to Humel. No, he must be a simple wanderer; must be. . . . So George is interested in something besides sex in Las Vegas. So what? Well, now I can see what, all right. Danger for me. An innocent bystander swept up in something, that is what. How have I got into this bind ... "between the devil and the deep blue sea," as her mother once said about Fiona's unfortunate color and the white community they lived in.

44

Here I am, same bind, between a rioting black area where I may find temporary cover if not slain outright and a white-and-yellow spy community where I cannot imagine when I may be killed or even for what reason.

It began last Saturday, only seven days ago.

PART TWO

5
Saturday, August 7.

It is only a week earlier and Fiona is cleaning house because George never comes on a Saturday. She has her hair protected from dust with a black chiffon scarf wrapped about her head. She is wearing jeans and a small-sized man's shirt of gray plaid from Sears. She has sneakers on so she can be sure not to fall climbing up and down the ladder to work on the black wrought-iron chandelier. She removes its chalk-white globes for a good soap-and-hot-water wash.

George appears at her side, or anyway, around her feet where they rest on the ladder at about his waist level. She all but drops a white glass globe to the floor. He has used his key to come in the kitchen door.

"Hi," she breathes on a shock wave. George is chewing at the side of his thumb, something he does only under stress. A phone call can bring on this kind of resort to nervous gnawing and gnashing at himself with his teeth.

48

"Hi," says George.

"I am just going to have a shower," says Fiona, coming down the ladder.

"No, no, can't stay," says George. "Just stopped by to confirm our flight tomorrow."

Why doesn't he use the phone as usual? This is queer. George moves to the window and, still gnawing, stares out at the wild front garden.

Fiona whips off the scarf and shakes her head to fluff out her hair.

"I am to be at the airport at eleven tomorrow, right?" she asks.

"Yeah. Say, we'll have all kinds of fun and games. You'll like Vegas," says George, slipping his hand in her shirt front to give her left breast a quick squeeze.

He moves toward the back door again. "So I'll see you," he adds, then opens the door and lets himself out.

What's this all about? I mean, in the first place there is this business of George asking her to go to Las Vegas with him. Has she been taken by George out of the house for dinner? Rarely, not to mention out of town, or even out of the state.

Is there a hint that George might even marry her, actually might marry her? Oh, this ridiculous, fleeting moment of marriage madness must be brought on by the excessive August heat; soft in the head, that's Fiona. Still, there's the encounter with the girl from Poland only last week. She meets her at the movies one afternoon and sits with her and her two children. Before the film they talk; they continue chatting at the intermission. The girl confides she's an ex-ballet dancer and a refugee from Poland. Now she has a large ballet school at Long Beach. Fiona must come for a weekend. Fiona is so happy with the attention from the girl, it is a moment of contentment. Fiona loves the young daughter's arm lying along the theater seat so close to hers; the skin is almost the same color and even darker. The husband and father must be very dark, but after the movie, when he calls for them and the girl introduces Fiona to him, she's amazed.

He is black, black as the ace of spades, black as her hat, a blackamoor. He's a physicist with a large corporation, the kind George works for. He's an American black too, born in the South, and gets out of it as a soldier, during the last war and afterward, the GI bill for college in Europe. Then he returns, an educated black with position and status.

But hell, George is no crusader. He's already got it made; he's safe in marriage; his children are born, both white, too, so they'll have that going for them if nothing more. Ah, well, she does entertain silly notions, but she isn't in love with George anyway. She's only in love with the idea of such safety for herself, a security she's never known. Secure in one's own person. What is that like? The ballet teacher, even in a mixed marriage, knows what that's like.

George, like all men of his stripe, will never give up having his cake and eating it too. This is what life for the aggressive is all about. Never mind, Fiona comforts herself, George won't marry me, and what's more, he'll tire of me before long. But there are plenty of men still out there and they're fully equipped with the same desires and plenty of money to buy it. George is even something of a bore, if truth be known, as it is to her.

Still, there is Las Vegas to look forward to—a change of scene, if only momentarily. Finish up the housecleaning; let's see, the wax for the furniture, then off to do some

50

shopping. There ought to be some things in the house by way of food for her return Monday afternoon, perhaps late.

Fiona takes a shower and dresses in an unobtrusive black silk and linen suit, a scarf with white polka dots at its neck. She locks the back door and walks little more than a block to the boulevard.

She seats herself on the edge of a bench that advertises Los Angeles funeral homes. She leans briefly against the large printing, "Foehn's Garden Park," and the slogan in script lettering, "In Remembrance of Those Past," and that is money business. She stands when she sees the Santa Monica bus coming fast upon her as though determined to squash her against the lamppost. She steps back a pace as it rocks to a brake-squealing halt, swishing air across her ankles.

She always has the exact fare ready to drop into the slot to keep conversation with "whites" to a minimum. She goes to the back of the bus to take a seat by herself and also to keep to a minimum any further complications to do with sharing a seat with a paleface. One cannot tell by looking from whom objections may come. Fiona does not want to antagonize anyone if planning ahead can avoid it. It is a matter of survival.

Downtown at Penney's she leaves the bus. She spots the shambling man following along behind her as she walks quickly along the street. She tests the situation to be sure she is not developing some kind of persecution complex. She pauses before the show windows featuring a crowded display of sleazy merchandise for sale to females to wear to a dog fight. Where else? Fiona thinks, gazing at the garish, flimsy muck.

She glances over her shoulder. Yes, he is pausing as well,

51

fascinated seemingly by a display of women's hats. Either he is following her or he has a peculiar fetish about head-gear for women. She tests him again by walking rapidly, then slowing up, then darting across the street, barely missing being hit when the red light flashes on. He keeps right up with her. She stops to gaze at the windows of the five-and-ten decorated with swim suits and caps.

She looks back and there he is, having a long look at a drugstore window filled with hot-water bottles, enema bags, and like items for the ailing; she will continue to pretend not to see him. She will think about packing her suitcase for Las Vegas this evening. Ignoring the man, she stares at a black swim suit, something like her own, only hers is three times more expensive. Slit at either side, low on the hips, with long bodice and short skirt; very smart, especially with her beige skin. Her swim cap is a tall bonnet with crown fluted about the top in feathery black flower petals.

He could be only a masher struck by her appearance. She wants him to be only that.

She'll ignore him. She looks at the caps. Hers is made in England and damned costly too, but worth every dollar because it keeps her hair completely dry and no frizzing. ... Let's see, she'll take the black toweling robe with the hood and . . . yes—she looks back quickly—yes, he still loiters behind her, not looking at her. She checks his billow-ing, poorly fitted brown suit. He's involved in this somehow, and stands now in a shop doorway only two stores away, picking at his teeth with a stout pick and looking toward the ocean to be seen glinting at the end of the street in the strong sunlight.

He is either very bad at his job or else doesn't care

whether she sees him or not. Why? Because he must know she is in the last position to complain to a cop. Maybe that's it.

Should she abandon this browsing tour before this large department store where she's planned to look about and step into this bus poised, with motor panting, here on the corner ready to take off? Before she makes up her mind, the driver swoops the bus out from the curb and into the rapid current of traffic, and as she stands there, she sees the bus come to a slashing stop at the next corner up the street.

But another bus rams into the space with a gigantic sigh of its power brakes. Quickly she runs up the steps, puts the change into the slot, and walks to the back.

She watches a third bus pull in right behind the one she is on, just as hers lurches up the street. This third bus pauses to discharge and take on more customers, but the man does not get on it. He steps into a taxi and follows along behind her bus. The taxi waits as the bus makes its stops.

No, this is not imagined. This is not another harmless admirer. The man is following her. Try to think. Hired by George's wife? Who else could have hired him? Her mother checking her out at this late date? What for? Her mother has no interest in her. Her mother will pay her a salary to stay the hell out of the way and even pay her to do anything she damned well pleases as long as it is conducted out of sight. Her mother, in fact, is still thrilled that Fiona has changed her name. No, her mother has nothing to do with this. She figures that she knows all there is to be known about her daughter Fiona. The stars tell her this, and so do Fiona's clothes, her ready cash, and her extensive travels.

Then it must be George's wife. But why Fiona? Why not

follow George? She won't mention any of this to George. Most wise to keep her own counsel. Maybe George will say something on his own.

Fiona sits on the bus and worries. Will the man jump her when she gets off at her stop? In the name of righteous George's wife? Wives! Smart ones can tell a threat a mile off. The threats even look like Fiona, except for color. George's wife ought to know Fiona isn't one of these young aggressive female types after a ring. Evidently she doesn't. Fiona would appreciate a chance to tell her. Because the competition is fierce, wives sometimes manage to hang on, but against terrible odds. The white Fionas are young, long of hair, toothy with smiles, joyous, slim of hip, long of leg. They wear gorgeous clothes and spend most of their available money on dressing the product, themselves, in the most appealing light.

Fiona looks like any of these young girls on the prowl for a husband. But there is a difference. They are free of charge to him until they get the ring; then they sell it and wield unlimited power. But Fiona trades straight across the board from start to finish. He pays and he gets.

Wives ought to adopt a like policy and cut the competition in half. Fiona can cheer them up, though, if they ask her; she can tell them just to remember that even these young things will have their turn at being old and spurned for an ever younger woman. Meanwhile, a male is a male from birth to death; age doesn't matter with a male.

The stock in trade of young seekers after a ring is the solemn single-minded aim to please. It is a studied, continuous production. A good reason why women dislike one another. They are aggregately second-class. They are nurtured to compete for identity borrowed from a husband.

54

They enter a contest for the pleased nod of commendation from the boss man, male. Slaves about the house and the plantation grounds dislike one another because they are all competing to be first in favor with the male white boss. It's a grim contest, and no sense in making friends among contenders.

Fiona often watches the wife competition in action in the Mar Vista dining rooms. Must get a husband to give me person, place, and things, lots of things; and a young girl on the make lowers her voice to an inaudible whisper so the man must bend closer to her and reap the full benefit of the exotic perfume she has sacrificed to buy. She is an operant type, a matter of conditioning and making use of reward and punishment like a wife; only Fiona and her ilk are one long reward with nary a whisper of punishment, not from them. Fiona is a success in her chosen profession.

But God, not today! She can write a loser's log today. Step back another space, Fiona, because it looks as though success can go to the bad at a moment's notice.

But, oh, tomorrow, Sunday, she'll fly off to Las Vegas. But why does George take her with him? Can it be a kind of gala, a fare-you-well? Fiona's swan song with George? There is something strange in the wind. She will do well to look sharp. Knives may be drawn for Fiona. A block before her stop, the taxi suddenly swerves away. An escort almost home, and then it is gone. Hell, don't think about it! Forget it.

6
Sunday, August 8.

Ah, at last they are to be seated in the one and only formal dining room of the giant gambling casino. There are many lunch counters of the ten-cent-store variety, but George won't have any of that.

The girl in the red, white, and blue Navy-inspired uniform that ends at her crotch—the flaring skirt covered with stars, stripes, and other pop art—takes George's order for Cutty Sark over plenty of ice and Fiona's Bacardi cocktail, not too sweet, please.

The girl returns on the double with the drinks and George tips her a dollar. When Fiona raises her glass, she sees over the rim a man who sits four tables away staring at her.

She lowers her drink. "There is a man over there watching us," she says.

George crouches over his glass, stirring the amber liquid about in the ice; he spins and whirls it about and looks from beneath his eyebrows in a belligerent stare. "Never saw the swine before. What's the matter with you? Edgy about something?"

56

Fiona eases herself over to the left on her chair, so that she is almost hidden from the man's sight.

"My God, Fiona, relax," says George. "You're acting like a nervous cat. About what?"

"Sorry, George. Maybe it was that fan jet taking off straight up in the air like that today and then wobbling around for a while until it got settled down. Then the landing here was another shock, straight down."

"Yeah, I got half a notion to put in a complaint on that. When a plane crashes, it's almost always pilot error. Some of these road jockeys squirreling around think they're driving a sports car on the salt flats."

No, this man can't even be a disliked acquaintance of the shambling man in brown who tailed her about Santa Monica yesterday; judging by appearance anyway, this is no bird of a feather. On the contrary, this one is neat, short, crisp; tidy hair, dark suit, dark tie, impeccable white shirt and, no doubt, beneath the table, well-polished shoes, loafers; clean socks in those and underneath it all clean shorts. He is rather like the men I pick out to pay for my living. She giggles, thinking it, and George all but snaps, "Now what? Hysteria?"

George is so short and brusque. What is wrong? Nothing bothers him as a rule. Well, to hell with him! Fiona takes a big gulp of the lovely-tasting drink and rolls it about her mouth. The ice is tiny and melts away to leave a dainty elixir of exquisite bouquet on her tongue. It warms her going down, and so gently. Yes, it is a fine drink. Maybe she'll have another to prepare herself to withstand the foul colors of their suite when they return to it. Deep purple, apple green, pink and black and gold all at once in their rooms. Another drink to withstand the entire layout, with its roulette wheels clicking away, crashing slot machines, and dirty paper cups underfoot.

There is a regular army of seedy little men in fresh white coats that make them look more seedy, trailing about twenty-four hours a day after pigs up on hind legs at all the tables and slots who drop everything they don't want —paper money wrappers, once firm with rolls of dimes and nickels; empty drink-on-the-house cups, and cigarette ash and butts too—all of it onto the thick carpeting beneath their feet. The little men sweep day in and night out, an army of white wingers, sweeping after the never-ending clutter strewn about the hoofs of sharp-faced, furrowed-of-brow speculators; the little men sweep on, handy little dust-pans on long handles in their hands.

Soon she'll be back in the black and gold and hot colors of the shiny Chinese suite, an ornate trim of near-brass on everything, and paper-thin walls through which this after-noon she hears every sneeze, cough, sigh, and giggle. She'll return to the bath lighting that gives her an aged, dated, and put-down-in-brine-for-pickles look—or, say, a victim of jaundice. To the place where the steady air conditioning flattens, sags, and dulls her hair, and also gives her a con-tinuous partial sore throat; where faucets are so modern and complicated she ought to have a telescope, and a pad and pencil to figure on, in order to calculate the steamed-over math formulas necessary to prevent herself from freezing or scalding to death in the shower, an ignoble way to die.

Fiona cuts her steak and prepares a tiny bite. An en-chantress with sunburned hay for hair drifts by their table. She wears a houri costume of gauze in orange and gold.

The pants suit on the fat lady makes her resemble a giant cloud. George gives her a filthy look and finishes his steak. He eats fast and with studied, undivided attention to the task at hand; he clears his plate tidily, and down all the years gone by back to his youth again, Fiona hears his mother say, "Polish that plate, George, or no dessert," and George still minds.

Now he has dessert—apple pie with cheese—and he takes gulps of coffee to wash it down. He lights a cigar and blows a cloud of smoke at Fiona's bosom as though marking it for future reference.

The man does not move. He smokes a cigarette and does not get up to go, even though refusing a refill of coffee. Then George stands, pulls the table back for Fiona, and the man gets up too.

Don't say anything further to George about this man; George is in a peculiar mood. He tips the waitress three dollars and pays the cashier.

"I'll walk you back to the rooms and check in later. Have some people to see. Okay?"

"I thought I might have a swim later on," she says.

"No; wait until tomorrow morning; I may be free by then," says George.

"Okay," says Fiona.

They walk back through the plastic, chrome, and highly colored Las Vegas casino; through the synthetic bleakness of it all, despite the frantic noise of high-rollers pretending they're having fun. The dreary sight of it depresses Fiona further. No more the hotel lobby, no more the long sofas, handy ashtrays, and chance to watch travelers going to and fro. Now the lobby is filled with solid rank on rank of slot machines and Keno players marking ballots with Chinese soft brushes dipped in black ink. They stand up to high desks, guessing and slashing away on the slips of paper, and keeping an eye out for their chosen numbers to flash up in lights on the big board near the ceiling. "Pay off big money, thousands of dollars," their eyes beg the board.

Oh, cheer up, Fiona, the value of the trip lies in how happy you'll be to be home again. She stands by the elevators. Looking out toward the gardens and swimming area, she watches George's back going down the long passageway.

The man from the dining room appears at his side. They shake hands. How funny! Why does George at dinner pretend not to know him, or has the man just introduced himself to George? Hell . . .

Alone in the room, Fiona listens to the canned music, this noise that goes on and on, everywhere, even in the elevator, the passageways; endlessly it plays, taped music grinding along night and day. Gay or plaintive music, dancing tunes, and already all of it has begun to sound so sad when not, in fact, asinine.

If I go shopping tomorrow morning, as I may do, then it will be heard in all the shopping centers as well. The tapes trill along over every sort of disaster: loss of home, or car, or both, at crap tables; terminal cases of cancer, here for what's left of health; they say the dry weather is good for the man she can hear coughing his lungs out next door. Maybe he's an exception.

Fiona snaps off the music, but she can still hear it through the walls, the door, and even in the bathroom, gay music spinning on and on, dispensing a mechanical song of well-being over snarling, lousy losers; plumbing rumbling and wailing in all the bathrooms, tribulation, travail, and stark terror—still the music goes on and on. . . . The telephone rings.

Fiona is stripping down to the skin. She steps from panty hose and picks up the receiver. George. Who else?

"Yes," Fiona says.

"George Aiken, please, long distance calling," says the operator.

"Call the desk, please," says Fiona. "This is the room maid."

"Room maid, my ass," says a man's voice. "Let me speak to her, whoever she calls herself."

"Go ahead, please," the operator says in her indifferent voice.

"Hello," says the man. "Listen, miss. Tell Aiken to call his boss," and the phone is slammed down with a bang in Fiona's ear.

She turns on the television and gets herself prepared and perfumed for George's return. If she ever gets back to her little house again, they'll have to carry her out of there bodily.

The newscaster is stating the case for a millionaire who owns much of Las Vegas. This rich man is daring the Atomic Energy Commission to set off its atomic bomb underground tomorrow morning at ten o'clock.

The newsman predicts the bomb will go off on schedule. It consists of the equivalent of thousands of tons of TNT. It will blast off on schedule, the newsman repeats. Not even this rich man has enough money to stop the boys from making a bang to help split the earth deeper.

A commercial comes on that is quiet, with no music or dialogue, and the whispering, busy, happy music comes from the hallway as George steps into the room.

Fiona is not going to be so stupid as to tell him about the long-distance call. She does not mix in his private affairs. It can only mean trouble for her.

George wishes to have everything done for him this evening. He appears to be exhausted. Perhaps he has been out to Yucca Flats, helping to make preparations for blowing up a piece of the globe.

Fiona wanders nude between bath and bed, priming George at the same time she makes ready. She calls Room Service for Scotch for George and rosé wine for herself. She lies on the bed spread-eagled and puts her arms above her head. George sits glumly in a chair.

When the waiter brings the drinks, George strips and gets into bed, leaving his shorts on. He props his head against the Chinese black-lacquer headboard, first placing a pillow there, and sips his drink. He looks a great over-sized long lump of a man. Fiona strokes his stomach and kisses him in light, barely brushing, tiny presses of her lips to his skin.

"Fiona, you're wonderful," says George.

He polishes off his drink, flicks out the light, and, turning over, rams himself inside her; Fiona clasps arms and legs about him to give him a full-value ride for his money. . . . George snores, and Fiona goes to the bath to wash and to wish it were tomorrow and time to go home.

George is gone early the next morning. Very odd! George is always interested in sex first thing in the morning before he leaves. Fiona dresses for breakfast.

In the dining room she watches all the people brooding sullenly over the hot coffee the snappy waitresses rush to supply. They look anxious to get into fun cars and planes, and leave to hell the mess behind them.

Two people at the next table are talking. "It's a new concept," says the first. "Yeah, tell it like it is," says the second.

Whine and snivel, and on they go about deprivation and cultural gaps. They wear little papers pinned to their chests on which their names are sloppily scrawled in red ink.

"What keeps me happy is being angry most of the time. . . ."

"It's a generation in search of a future. . . ."

They'll get over all that too, Fiona thinks, like an oracle; this, too, will pass away. Fiona checks all the diners. The watching man of last night is not among them. . . . Maybe she ought to take a walk. . . .

She finishes her coffee and roll. She steps outside where it is most of all gritty, and soft with melting tar along the edges of the roadway before the casino. The wind blows, the sun glares, and soon there will be earth tremors when the little boys with their shiny new toys make a bigger bang than the one before.

She hails a taxi and leaves it promptly near a dress shop sporting a long green and white awning before it. She tries on rapidly—and takes off just as swiftly—a series of the tacky modern clothing being shown. She is soon exhausted by this silly exercise of skimming on and off all the stuff that looks so rotten anyway. She buys a large straw hat for the garden—in beige, in defiance of the clerk who remarks that, with her skin, perhaps she ought to choose the other color, which is brown. Actually, she likes the long paisley scarf tied around it.

She pays for a beige overblouse to wear with cocoa linen slacks and leaves the shop clutching a paper sack with smart lettering in red down its middle. "Elizabeth's Shop," the writing reads.

Farther along, she steps into a larger store and selects a terra-cotta lipstick that makes her think the dead-looking color has captured all the essence of synthetic Las Vegas in its hue, a kind of silvery-shit color. Hell.

Now she can't resist twelve white linen napkins, with a fat embroidered initial J in one corner of each of them. So elegant! And in minutes the clerk has them awash in crisp tissue paper, and packed carefully in a flat box.

Fiona picks up a tiny pillbox scrolled in twisted gold, from India, and adds it to her loot; and finally, a sword letter-opener with hilt in a scabbard of leather—just in case she gets a letter to open, or perhaps she can murder George with one thrust of it into his stout heart and make all the newspapers at once.

She'll wear the linen suit on the trip home, with the white beret because her hair looks so terrible. Out in the hot sun, Fiona eyes a tennis racquet in the window of a sporting goods shop next door. She goes in and fingers the ridiculous item, buys it, and asks herself who will play tennis with Fiona, "All Love," out in the broad daylight? The heat has melted her brain as it has the hot tar in the street. Thirty dollars for a tennis racquet, and she swings it back and forth at her side and hopes a taxi will come along soon. She will fly away home right now if the opportunity presents itself. But it won't, not until George is ready. Even in the frightening fan jet, even with that to get her home, yes, even so, she'll go. So much for wishful thinking, tennis racquets, and going home.

64

She is melting in the sun. There is not a sign of a cruising taxi. She'll have to call one. Oh, right over there is a shady-looking garden nursery; only a few steps and she can be inside an arbor with wide-open redwood gates. Inside, it is almost cool by contrast—or looks it—and quiet and peaceful too. The street-traffic noise dims and there before her are two Greek cypress trees—so dark black and green and slim and tall and elegant—planted in olive tubs. Laced about their trunks at the bottom is a pool of sparkling white rock. How lovely they would be on either side of her front door at home! Yes, as though she might need to open the door to welcome in ordinary, friendly folks; even a salesman, someone to speak to in the daytime. Fiona, grow up; you won't be welcoming even a friendly salesman at your front door if you're smart.

How silly to contemplate! Besides, they are funeral trees, death and memorial trees, and ought at least to stand like sentinels at the corners of a marble reflecting pool, before a white stone villa in Italy or someplace.

Fiona drops the sack and looks at the once-chalk-white glove on her left hand. The smart sack with the elegant English script dancing down its length has sweated its cheap red paint all over the glove that has clutched it, and the heat has finished the job. Damn.

Get back to the hotel and into the swimming pool, George there or not. She can't wait. Why did she buy the stupid hat anyway? A sun hat, for a person who worries about tanning too much. What a laugh! Well, of course, it can spare her eyes from squinting in the sun glare. . . . Ah, at last a taxi bowling along. She hails it and soothes herself with thoughts of getting into the black swim suit and into the pool.

Fiona seats herself by the pool in a lounge chair laced with copper nylon and puts the black duck bag with its smart white-rope drawstring on the table. She sits beneath an umbrella and pulls on the black swim hat. She pushes up inside it at the back all the hot steamy hair, and already that is some relief.

The pool is empty except for a very dark-brown lifeguard who appears to be asleep beside the pool at the far end. He lies flat on his face, arms clasped about his head, and the music plays on and on as Fiona jumps into the water, enjoying the shock of its delicious coolness all over herself all at once.

She swims back and forth countless times, then turns over to float on her back and stare at the brassy hot sky.

She climbs out and puts on the terry short coat and the new hat on her head against the glare. She lights a cigarette and sits dripping in contentment in the shade of the copper umbrella.

Now what is the peculiar chill in the air? Why do the trees appear to glitter, their leaves shimmering as though seized by a nervous ailment? They twist and writhe in a dancing, trembling shock wave when there is not a sign of a breeze. What can this be? A black cloud moves over the sun. The white face of the sturdy building appears to shimmer into movement too. A building quivering? What is happening? The underground explosion? The lifeguard sits up. He leaps into the deep corner of his end of the pool, douses himself up and down, gets out and lies flat again, this time on his back.

Fiona takes her watch from her bag and straps it on. It is five minutes after ten. Now the sensation of movement is gone; everything is normal. The sun streams down, turning the hair on the back of her neck to steaming spirals.

A man comes through the gate and straight to her side. He wobbles when he walks, then stands before her. "I am a Norwegian," he tells her. "Listen, they play a Strauss waltz." He hums with it and sways. "Will you dance with me?"

"No thanks," says Fiona.

"How about a smoke?"

"No thanks."

"Say, how about a drink?" he asks as a black man walks along outside the fence. "Say, boy," the Norwegian shouts and runs to the gate. "Here's a couple of bucks for you. Send a waiter out here; the lady and I can use a drink."

"Okay, boss," the young man says and continues on his way. "Thank you," he adds over his shoulder with a faint smile.

The handsome drunk begins to tell Fiona about his life, starting with his wife, then to his lousy job, on to the people he knows in show biz, as he calls it. "You take Buddy Muller, I mean he goes back to L.A. last night, and he's running to fat; don't take care of himself the way I do. Here, have a feel of that muscle."

Fiona does not move. She smokes and says nothing.

The man runs down. "Say," he asks her, "where do you think that guy went I gave the money to? I mean, where's the waiter?"

Fiona is packing up her things.

"Say, who do you think you are, so damned uppity stuck up, about what?" he asks.

When they blow up the world, I am hounded by a drunk. . . . Back to more of the monstrous Chinese suite; anything is better than this.

"Fiona," George calls from outside the fence, "let's go."

"Your keeper is whistling, black bitch," says the drunk.

Fiona moves toward the gate.

"Goddamned nigger whore," the man adds, dropping himself into the pool, shoes and all. The lifeguard comes running with rule book in hand.

George is waiting and chewing at his thumbnail. "Want to get that first flight back. Didn't think you'd be hanging around the pool."

"I was alone until the drunk came," says Fiona.

"Well, let's get packed."

At the airport Fiona asks, "Did you have a nice time, George?"

"Sure, even took a sauna this morning."

That's a lie. Why?

Fiona dreads the takeoff in the fan jet, but she is so glad she's going home she can't even worry about that. On board the plane, the stewardess wears a smart blue and yellow shift frock with a swift four inches of skirt to it. When she bends over the man in the seat across the aisle from them, it makes Fiona giggle because she is thinking that there is competition of the "take it off" variety everywhere and, what is murder for Fiona types, it's free—well, for the moment it's being given away free.

She takes a gulp of whiskey and icy soda and resolves to go to a play, a show, anything, this evening, all by herself. To hell with irritable hulk George.

At International Airport in Los Angeles, George hands her a luggage check at the foot of the ramp, saying, "I'll get back to you."

"Thanks," says Fiona, all business and eyes wary.

7
Monday, August 9.

At home, Fiona thrills to be in the dead silence of her house. Haven at last! She skims off the beret and sails it to the sofa; she sits, leans back, folds her hands, alone, calm, and at peace.

The back doorbell peals with such a loud insistent shriek in the dead quiet of the house that Fiona jumps. She jerks to her feet and goes through the house. She opens the door to a workman who looks as though he spends not one penny to replace or even wash his clothing. He grins at her, displaying a toothless lower gum. He runs his eyes up and down her neatly clad figure in the smart suit.

"Yes, what is it?" Fiona asks.

"Yer landlord says for me to come by to let you know I'll do some tarring repairs up on the roof tomorrow."

"He hasn't called me."

"Says he did and can't reach nobody."

"Oh," says Fiona.

Reasonable enough, since she hasn't been here. Also, the landlord does have her unlisted number that is in her mother's name, Epts. A little future surprise for her perhaps.

. . . Why is she doing all this thinking about a simple enounter with an ordinary workman? Nerves again?

"You been outta town?"

"Yes," says Fiona.

"Well, it's a dirty mother of a job," says the workman, a paleface, spitting now into the rosebush at the left of the back door. The sun gilds his spittle and turns the slobber to gold, silver, and every hue of the rainbow.

"Yes," says Fiona, starting to close the door.

"I won't be in yer way from that angle," he goes on. "Just up on the roof spreading some hot tar, patching around. You had any leaks?"

"No," says Fiona.

"Well, you probably got them termites around them chimneys anyway," he says while his eyes smirk at Fiona's bosom in the white linen blouse.

"Yes. Excuse me," says Fiona, closing the back door.

Shall she call the landlord and check this stranger out? Oh, what else can he be besides a roof patcher? On this score one look convinces anyone in his right mind.

Who says I'm in my right mind? So plan what to do with the rest of today and tomorrow and ease your mind. It is the only thing to allay these feelings of nerves, panic, and even heart-thumping at the slightest contact with anyone at all. Calm down, she counsels herself, and set up a routine. Let me see . . . what to do to keep the red devils of doubt and fear from driving their pitchforks further into the brain. Distraction, diversion for the rest of today and tomorrow. Don't forget there is tomorrow. It could be worse.

Walk it off, walk miles. In daylight it is almost safe for walking, even for the black and female. Not much selective law enforcement and rousting going on in the daytime, not

70

if one walks fast, businesslike, with purpose. And Monday is a work day.

She puts her beret on again, picks up the suit coat and handbag, and locks the back door. She leaves her sanctuary briskly and without reluctance, as though it has quite suddenly become a trap. Frightened off like a simpleton by the brief contact with a roof patcher.

A little way down from her house two women engage in whispers at her approach. Fiona looks far too smart for the court. They hang over a dividing fence and chatter more loudly as she draws near, then fall silent as she passes.

"No visible means of support," one of them calls after her.

"Not much," says the other. "Begin with her shape. She's got visible means, all right."

To hell with them. Fiona stares ahead, chin high, back ramrod straight. She clips her heels along the center paving of the court, which is rotting along its edges.

Why does George pretend not to know the man in Las Vegas? Why, in fact, does George make a show of being testy about Fiona's noticing the watchful, well-dressed man who is staring at them? George acts ruffled about a perfect stranger to him, a person he later greets and shakes hands with, after he thinks Fiona is in the room. What sense does this make? It is suspicious to know someone, and not simply say so and go on to something else. Fiona doesn't give a damn if George knows anyone or not. He must know hundreds. Who cares? Why make such a thing of it? Too bad the man doesn't turn out to be simply another potential and innocent customer. Yes, too bad, because Fiona feels she can give George the gate and take the other man on overnight. This is how she feels about troublemaker George right this minute.

But no, this man is no doubt someone far more sinister, with implications for Fiona of nothing but danger. Just the memory of his watching shark eyes gives her a creepy feeling.

Up on the corner, just before reaching the boulevard, Fiona sees the little bulldog woman marching about her garden in all but military cadence. She reminds Fiona of a French policeman taking full charge of fearful traffic snarls. The little paleface snaps herself left and right and all about her yard. As a rule, when Fiona nears the woman's gate, she darts behind a tree and then leaps out to shout a loud-voiced, "Hello there, Miss."

Today, as always, Fiona jumps at this startling greeting, but manages a soft hello in return. Still, the woman speaks to her, no matter how unexpectedly or loudly.

Two blocks down from Seconna Place, Fiona passes the cut-rate drugstore. She'll pick up a paperback and some candy for this evening at home. After making her selections, she stands in a long line to pay the cashier. She is just behind a large, fat, black woman of about fifty, who holds a large, cracked, plastic purse in a cracked, swollen, knuckled hand. She scrabbles desperately inside the bulging purse for more money. The selected sleazy bits of baby clothing, diapers, and shirts rest on the counter between her and the clerk. The clerk's right eye is turned inside out with an affliction of some kind that has left it beet-red, raw, and wet. Gaping and tipped over, the eye fixes the old black woman with an impatient and highly dramatic glare. The old woman scratches on through her purse, dipping inside zipper compartments, pockets, and slits. Then several withered-looking coin purses are gone through. Finally she delves deep into a large shopping bag she carries on her arm. Those behind Fiona, waiting to be served, press closer, sigh, and change position to another slouch. Not one of the crannies will produce enough coins to pay the amount indicated so authoritatively in large red numbers in the window of the register.

Fiona, out in the white world where who knows what may strike next, has two dollar bills in hand, ready to slap down with proper attention to restraint and humility before the gaping, bloody eye of the cashier. Now she places one of these in the last coin purse in which the defeated old woman roots by way of delaying the announcement that she hasn't enough money.

The old woman glances in disbelief at Fiona and, wondering and grateful, she hands the bill to the clerk, who takes it snappily, slaps it beneath a wire holding a thick stack of bills, taps out change on her computer register, and makes a show of putting out her hand for Fiona's money.

Fiona hands her a five and the old woman waits to say thank you. She asks if she can have Fiona's address so that she can repay her.

"No," says Fiona, "it's my pleasure, if you don't mind."

Fiona steps into a bus for the two-mile ride from Venice to Santa Monica. At the back of the bus she takes a seat and takes the tiny mirror from her handbag to make lipstick repairs she ought to have done before leaving her house in such a hurry. It is slovenly to make a public application of make-up.

Unaware, she opens the first case she comes to at the bottom of the purse. She opens it to the silvery shit-color lipstick symbolic of the plastic essence of Las Vegas, if not a synthetic symbol of her entire life. . . . I am not running; I am only diverting myself. It's the survival of the fittest and the tough. To hell with crumpled old ladies without enough money; most of all, to hell with George. She can use this lipstick in the backyard to keep her lips from chapping. The workman is a workman, period. Who else could he be in those clothes?

In Santa Monica she changes to a Wilshire bus and stays on it while it fights traffic for eighteen miles. She leaves it at Vermont in Los Angeles. She begins to walk in the park, enjoying the sight of a large black dog cooling itself in the public fountain, wallowing and shaking itself when it leaves the water to trot down the marble stairs. Look sharp, Fiona. Police arrest citizens in this area if they have the undesirable look; you've got it, all right. Black, female, alone.

Sometimes the police turn the park over to nature without the clutter of human feet simply by causing the sprinklers to be turned on, and leaving them on until the park is flooded and can be enjoyed only by ducks. Anyone in power knows the ends always justify the means. Benches have been spirited away too. No longer can old useless men sit drooling pleasurably at young office girls on their way to lunch. The ducks, however, are still in residence and waddle along, picking up droppings and soiling the paths and walks so that young office girls gripe about ruining their best shoes slipping and sliding in duck feces. But authorities point out the park is clear of undesirable persons and that is the main idea.

Fiona skirts the soiled spots on the walks and rubs her eyes turning red from the smog. She won't frequent this area longer in her elegant suit because selective law enforcement can well bring on her arrest on charges of wearing an undesirable color of skin. Move on.

She walks beside a high school, behind a group of young

boys and girls wearing their hair shoulder length. She marvels at the glossy good looks of the boys' hair that has never been long before, never has known permanents, bleaching, or dyes; it has a just-born look. She can see why the boys find it attractive; so does she. By comparison, it is easy to pick out the girls, with their abused, teased, or ironed hair. Fiona stares at the fashions. Today, style has become the great social leveler. Everyone, rich and poor and in between, can look alike. It's the tacky time of fashion. Everyone in style because it's all that's shown for those with money to buy, and those with little can get the same thing at the Salvation Army.

There's the old patchwork quilt of velvet pieces Fiona buys for two dollars at the Good Will. She can remove the padding and put in a new silk lining. What a lovely right-to-the-floor evening skirt she'll have to greet George. It looks like a stained-glass window with its reds, blues, and browns, all muted with time. And subtle. Yes, it's lovely, and stitched about the patches with black, too. Perhaps she'll start it tomorrow.

She walks along the edge of a private and expensive California university, a school for the privileged. Carefully she avoids the eyes of the paleface rich who pass her, these carefree scions and heiresses of the wealthy.

But now the tide of black color washes close to its exclusive shores, it laps about the very fences of this school. Fiona meets face after face of coal black and they examine her closely, unlike the few-and-far-between palefaces, who show no recognition that anyone has gone by at all. The black faces give Fiona a feeling of security. What will this college do when the black tide of color swallows it up? Something soon, because the tide seeps closer day by day.

It will pick up its power and money and move, that's what.

A large sign reads "Housing Exhibition." Why not go inside and have a look? Fiona pays the one dollar and fifty cents entrance fee and strolls along before all the shell-room interiors ranging the walls inside.

The cutaways of ideal rooms are filled with low, sprawling, overstuffed chairs and sofas in a variety of pop-art colors. There are many ornate and gilded accessories strewn about on tiny box tables of glass and metal, or squared and boxy wood tables painted in primary colors like cubes for a kindergarten. Fat draperies of splashy puffed patterns hang at fake windows. Gigantic lamps so high up a person hoping to read beneath their light will need to stand to get close enough to the bulbs far above him.

Outside again, Fiona sees more and more black faces thronging the sidewalks. Yes, it is soothing. She ought to move here. But who would come to see her here? George and his kind of paleface, with money for Fiona, won't come here. Not likely. No, she must stay in the Caucasian ghetto. But isn't it lovely, the secure feeling, no matter how fleeting, of walking along a sidewalk predominantly walked by persons with dark faces? A nice change, to blend with passers-by.

Fiona enters a small café, a black café. She sits at the counter and orders the supper of the day. They cook hot, these Southern chefs; the beans burn and scour her throat all the way to her stomach; her insides feel on fire, but what a fiery lift to her spirits! She can see why blacks pepper their food, perhaps as a counterirritant, and think about their insides on fire while diverting their thoughts from fires without that may come to them from any side at any moment.

76

Ah, here is the Shrine auditorium, and now at dusk people buy tickets to see the opera company's performance of "Otello." She will really enjoy this. Why not go?

Fiona joins the line and buys a ticket right down in the front row before the orchestra. She is seated so close to the man singing the Otello role, she can feel his flying slobber spray her face when he exerts himself at his most thunderously dramatic.

Fiona is almost happy. It is thrilling. She is right inside the story, right up there among them on the stage. Iago, how she detests him, this bear-baiter; Otello, how compassionate she feels for him. She is taken out of herself in the rousing drinking scene; she even feels sympathy for the blue-eyed blonde in her prayer scene. When Otello strangles her, Fiona is shocked but—she's happy. She ignores the man next to her nudging her arm and staring. At intermission she says a firm no to his invitation. She has no interest in lemon squash. She stays right where she is so as not to lose the feeling of being in another world. She is part of the story going on up there.

At the finish of the opera, when she leaves the Shrine auditorium to catch the Wilshire bus for Santa Monica again, her mind is almost at ease. She sits on the bus still lost in the opera's beauty. She does not even notice the gradual replacement of black faces by white. The closer she comes back home to the sea and the farther away from Los Angeles downtown, the more the whites take over. When she prepares to get off at Santa Monica, she is the only black left on board.

After midnight, and she has the good sense to get right into a taxi. The paleface at the wheel is as polite as he needs to be, and pleases Fiona by saying nothing except "Thanks" when she hands him three dollars for the one-seventy-five-cent fare home. Her life style, whatever else it may be, is, above all, expensive.

At one in the morning, Tuesday, Fiona is in bed, but she has Tuesday planned too. She goes to sleep satisfied and bone tired after the evening out. She is relaxed and off guard and can't suspect in a million years what will start off her day when she opens the door in the morning. Who can fathom ahead of time such an oddity?

PART THREE

8
Tuesday, August 10.

By nine o'clock Fiona is ready to leave her tidy house to the tar man and any other suspect or ordinary manifestations to come upon it. She unlocks the back door and stoops over all the rolled, folded, and wadded-up clutter of thrown-away newspapers accumulated there.

The unwanted papers contain page after page of advertising. The ads vie for attention from prospective buyers, and shopkeepers suggest they are set to all but throw away everything in their stores, or in any event to sell it for mere pennies compared to its actual worth. The papers decorate all the yards in the entire area every Tuesday. If not picked up, they multiply, and within three weeks of a householder moving on, great mountains of the yellowing promotional papers stack up in all directions.

As Fiona picks up the last bundle of her own to put in

the garbage can, a tiny, curled around, and stiffened kitten falls onto her back step. A curious and cruel manifestation. She hopes it is only her nutty, paleface neighbors playing little tricks to pass their time. They wish me to move, perhaps.

The kitten is stone still in death. Its paws curl helplessly before itself as though in prayer. Its neck is withered because it has been strangled. Fiona strokes its black silky fur and permits one tear to roll down her beige cheek. She touches the chalk-white forefoot, so soft, round, and untried.

Still so lovely, even dead. The kitten's mouth is drawn back, showing tiny picket teeth, and as Fiona puts it down, tiny white maggots in a small writhing ball tumble from the stiff lips. In her neat navy blue suit Fiona takes a shovel to dig a small grave. She brings a clean white dish towel from the house and rolls the body into the shroud. She covers it over and places stones over the tiny mound it makes.

Who leaves her this message? Not George's wife. It must be a neighborhood mad person. People about here are middle-aged, and most marked deeply by depression when young. Blighted and scarred at a tender age and grown, still blighted, to middle age. They are mean.

With other so-called higher types of the same age bracket firm in the saddle of authority and leadership, there can't be a worse time for blacks to choose to make a stand for first-class citizenship. Authorities bred in depression are mean; oh, they are very mean, indeed!

Fiona washes her hands. What's left to come to her these peculiar days? A few harassing phone calls, if anyone can stumble upon her number. This will complete the siege.

Some calls are marked only by the sound of heavy, menacing breathing when she lifts the receiver. Others, young pranksters, call to say, "Fuck you," and on one occasion Fiona replies, "It will cost you." Does it relieve pent-up hates for those who make these shock calls to strangers as they mumble something in their slimy sick voices? Poor saps, wriggling from beneath rocks, oozing filth, and sliding quickly down into their dark places once more!

Why hasn't George called? This is odd. . . . And this added oddity, this fortunate rather than unlucky very dead kitten. She thrills at this kitten's good luck at being dead and so escaping the hell that would await it otherwise.

Fiona can hear the sound of scraping and bumping as a ladder is placed against the side of the house. It is the man with his tar brush. She can hear brushing noises on the roof and he is singing something in happy, gusty shouts. She can't wait to spend the entire damned day out of her haven again. She will go to the library and pick up a stack of books, and have lunch out, and pick up some liquor on the way back. She may even take a stroll through the boulevard nursery and stare at the peaceful trees and flowers, and not return until late. And then maybe George will call.

The man is lashing himself about with his bucket of hot tar in one hand and his brush in the other. He is howling out a mad tune, a jolly-sounding shout, except Fiona can hear the words plainly. "Oh, you dirty little old son of a mother bitch," he sings, "I'd like to smash your frigging face . . . oh ho ho, ha ha, oh you . . ." and caroling and chortling along. Fiona watches two ladies smile in fine indulgence at the sound of the song of a happy workman. They can't hear the lyrics and besides, Fiona is black, so if they could, the words are good enough for her.

84

Fiona walks swiftly away up the court to the boulevard and bus stop. She comforts herself that the hot tar will get some of the termites. If they are living about the chimneys, how long will it be before they are down inside the house boring into the wood of her closet, making their turrets and towers of sawdust?

At the public library Fiona goes directly back into the stacks to select the four books she is permitted to take out at one time.

Slowly and with reluctance she approaches the check-out desk. She waits behind a woman who is a friend of the librarian.

"Yes, I'm off at last to Arrowhead around the first of September," the friend says.

"My, you'll have fine weather for it, and not so crowded," says the librarian.

"We have our own cabin."

"How nice."

"We never rent it. Tenants do too much damage."

"That keeps out some people too."

"Yes, much more exclusive, and an excellent group; only our regulars."

"Of course you get tourists, but they must come and go."

"We don't make it attractive enough for them to linger."

"Catalina used to be so nice."

"Oh, it's gone to rack and ruin, everyone going there."

"Yes, most of the regulars have gone."

"Far better in the mountains. I like the high elevation; makes you feel peppy."

"But no swimming?"

"Yes indeed, we have swimming pools. We're just like a big family, together all the time, sharing it all."

Fiona shifts her books to the other arm. The librarian can't see her. She looks right through Fiona. Fiona is empty space. Her body is a dusky screen through which the woman can see long tables at which people bend over books or whisper discreetly to one another.

The woman turns and says "Oh," and then, "Well, I'll see you later, Lillian. Try to get up to us."

"Will do, Betty. Thanks," and she puts out her hand to take Fiona's books, as though Fiona has been holding her up.

Carefully, so as not to touch fingers and offend, Fiona places the books on the counter before her and stands back a space to wait. Gingerly the woman examines the card Fiona has placed on top of them. It's another surprise for her mother someday. Fiona Epts, it reads, her real name. Of course the address is a lie. The librarian flops the book covers open in a stack, removes the cards, shoves them into a machine for stamping, snaps them back into the book pockets, slaps the books closed, and pushes the lot toward Fiona, who says thanks and walks away.

The woman hasn't said one word to Fiona; maybe her supply is exhausted after her exchange with Betty.

At what point do these trivial slights and scars become deep wounds? At no point, because it's more like the wearing away of rock by water. A gradual affair, Fiona is thinking as she enters the restaurant. The girl with menus assigns her a table for one by the swinging doors to the kitchen. Fine, maybe the waitress will be in a better mood if she does not have to walk so far to serve Fiona.

The waitress stands beside her, ruffling the pages of the order pad. Fiona waits until bidden to speak.

"Yes?" the girl inquires.

"A grilled cheese sandwich and lemon Coke, please," says Fiona.

The girls says nothing. She marks it down in slashing script on the stained pad. She snaps the menu up from Fiona's place, pockets the pad, and goes to the counter where she squirts Coke, fizz, and a dash of lemon over an ice cube. She raps it down before Fiona and disappears into the kitchen. Fiona's Coke is almost gone when the girl serves the half-cold sandwich. The chef has been given the message: "A nig." Eat someplace else, girl. Eat these worms, Fiona, and remember who you are: nothing, a prostitute, and black, and female. So swallow it.

Two ladies at a nearby table eye Fiona's smart appearance. One says, loudly enough to show Fiona how little she cares if Fiona hears her because who cares about this no-competition-stuck-with-that-skin person, "Colored. My husband says he can tell by their funny protruding heels."

"She is quite good-looking; well dressed, too," says her friend.

"I know. That's what makes you mad. You can see them all over driving their big cars. We drive a Ford."

"She's got a lot of white blood," says the woman with resentment, as though she is in charge of that.

The ladies collect gloves, handbags, and numerous crackling sacks of merchandise, charge slips stapled to the tops of them from nearby shops, while Fiona restrains herself from indulgence in the passing whim to upset the remains of their cold coffee down their fronts.

Fiona enters the gate of the garden nursery and the Oriental owner greets her. "Good afternoon, Miss."

"Good afternoon. Will you send me twelve of those white

petunia plants, please? And I'll take twelve of those small pots, please."

The tiny man with the wizened yellow face moves delicately on tiny feet to round up her order for delivery. Fiona also chooses a can of white spray paint from the large selection available. She will busy herself at home tomorrow whether the house is besieged, haunted, or what. And whether George calls or whether . . . what the hell!

She ought to ask the little man for black pots and black flowers. God should have made them all black, but he made lots of white, because black is for death, of course. Lilies ought to be black.

Fiona, shaking off the gloom, goes on to the grocery store and comes out juggling the books and a tall sack she cannot very well see over or around. She has eggs, cheese, apples, oranges, ham, and the books. . . .

The shock of her fall resounds in her ears and rings on and on like disturbed bells. She has tripped over the narrow lip of concrete in the aged sidewalk. Stunned, she watches oranges roll to the gutter. She lies on her stomach before the eyes of two men eating at the quick-lunch diner on the corner. She pulls herself to her feet as the men come out arguing about the taxes they are required to pay for these deteriorating public walks. They go off, still arguing, and climb into their cars and roar away.

Fiona, limping, picks up some of the groceries. The torn sack won't hold them all, so she leaves most of the oranges and apples behind.

She favors the left leg now because the right knee is cut and is bleeding. She bleeds bright red down the beige of her leg. Shall she go on to see her kindly Jewish doctor or take care of it herself at home with the same kind of ointment her mother once kept on hand? Heal it up quickly though, because men don't like their women bruised and torn. They like sleek, elegant women who appear physically perfect, or at least whole. Fiona giggles in spite of the pain from the knee that cracks open each time she takes a step.

With two blocks to go from her turn-off into the court, Fiona enters the liquor store on the corner. Then she can take that short cut home across an empty lot and save some walking, even though she detests the place where cats prowl, dogs fight, and Mexicans, Africans, and Chinese get drunk and beat up one another. The lot is all but solidly strewn with broken glass, an area of broken dreams. When liquor-store customers finish their bottles, they crash them to pieces on the rocky ground in splendid imitation of the swells in the movies who toss delicate crystal glasses into the stone of mammoth fireplaces. There is a red line drawn about this district by the insurance companies and anyone residing inside must pay higher rates. Burglars pay almost weekly calls on those in the neighborhood who might have something stashed away, but mostly they count on the punch-drunk owner of the liquor store for a weekly haul.

"Hi," he says to Fiona. He is always friendly to her and does not seem to care what color she is, or what she does for a living, or perhaps his brains are too addled by all the gun-carrying robbers to know. His visiting hijackers always pistol whip him as a matter of operation and good form, and one time they even locked him up in his own back storeroom for good measure, among the boxes of corn flakes and soap he sells on one side of the shop.

"Hursh your lag?" he asks Fiona in sympathy. His speech is slurred both from sampling his own wares and from his disastrous brushes with abrasive robbers. But this is an abrasive neighborhood anyway. Sheriff's deputies make regular calls to dun citizens for overdue bills, and the gas company makes scheduled trips to turn off gas of customers lagging in payments.

"Only a scrape," says Fiona, picking out a bottle of Cold Duck wine. George likes it with a midnight supper sometimes. The kindly shopkeeper takes all her groceries, her library books, and the bottle of wine and places them compactly inside two sacks. Fiona pays him and picks up the double sacks to leave.

"Thash pretty heavy for a lil girl. Lemme bring it for you when I lock up for slupper," slurs the man in his blurred speech, wavering behind the cash register as though standing in a strong wind.

"Thanks very much," says Fiona, "but I can manage. I'll go slow."

Outside, Fiona crackles along, picking her way carefully over the shards and chips of glass. Perhaps George will call this evening, she will have things ready for a supper, just in case he does decide to come by. Her number is listed on the calendar card George carries in his wallet. A lousy memory for a math man? A psychological blank of some kind? Doesn't wish to remember her number? Beside her number on the calendar card he has the word GARAGE printed. That is good. Fiona is a garage all right, for his sword.

It is late, she thinks; about ten o'clock. She can't see the little crystal and gold clock over there on the dressing table. She lies on the bed with the orange light casting a luminous glow on the gossamer sheer gold of the nightdress she wears. Her knee is bandaged discreetly, only a small dressing covers the wound. She reads Froude's "Life and Letters of Erasmus"; "From argument, there would be a quick resort to the sword and the whole world would be full of fury and madness." Two hundred years of war over religion proved him right. . . .

Why doesn't George call? . . . Is someone looking at her? She feels the tingling sensation of being watched. She glances up to the tiny window over the closet where she has not drawn the curtain because her knee aches when she limps about before going to bed. So few people bother to peek in this immediate area anyway; they have other things on the mind; money, mostly.

Yes, there he is. From the side he looks like a rooster. The one eye she can see is placed conveniently for him on the side of his knife face. His hair sticks up from his tall head like a cockscomb. His mouth works as though snapping at hard chick seeds. She pretends she doesn't see him. His profile is pressed so close to the glass that through her thick eyelashes she can see him plainly. His prominent nose is a beak and his cheek looks stuck to the window glass. The one eye continues to swivel up and down her figure. She feels an odd desire to giggle. She reaches up and snaps off the light. She moves to the window, climbs on a chair, and pulls the curtains closed.

His footprints will be plain beneath the window tomorrow, but she hasn't the nerve to check out there now. And what for? He is three gardens away by now. If he isn't, what can she do? Call the cops? Hold him?

She examines the back-door lock, especially for George's key. Well, he will have to ring if he comes late tonight. Because she snaps the night lock and chains the door as well.

What would it be like to call the servants of the other people, the police? They are not her servants; they are her masters. The country is now another and a larger Vietnam. It's a riotous, violent country. Perhaps it is being punished in turn for the punishment given to Vietnam.

Fiona shivers and wishes someone would lie close to her. Hell, she is surely not upset at this weirdo looking at her. He can't get in and only wishes to look anyway. He is probably not capable of anything else, poor slob, poor old rooster. . . .

Will this country ever try to appease the aspirations of the oppressed? Does any country ever toss more than a sop? No. Costs too much. It will try to put rebellion down by force. The use of force is disaster. That will cost more, and not in coin. (She's getting too much like her mother, predicting things she knows nothing about. Maybe she can be a fortune-teller in her old age.) Every emancipation is only the start of another form of slavery anyway. But what if Fiona had been born free? The truth shall make you free, not crippled for life, humiliated day in and day out by perfect strangers, the women at the library, in the café. What might it have been like to have had a taste of some kind of emancipation from birth? And what if any truth becomes a lie? Well, she might not be here tonight, wincing away from the very thought of the bleak prospects strung out before her like grave markers, with fingers shaking at her warning of dire things to come.

This is a country ruled by force and the military; a nation of laws, not men; and Fiona's on the bottom, hasn't got a prayer. Maybe the country has a hope in the unruly, rebelling college kids. Or maybe they only act up because they feel guilty at being privileged to stay out of Vietnam.

92

Or maybe they raise hell with the old order because they are honestly idealistic. Or maybe they have a vested interest, an interest in preserving the world long enough for them to live out their allotted life span. In any case, these scions of the swells with their revolt are the only hope the country has left. Will the leaders believe that? Of course not. What's in it for them personally? That question comes first and last. That Bible stuff about a little child leading them, all that bull! Don't be daft. Someday there won't be anything left to fight over and then maybe the leaders might believe.

The telephone rings. Fiona eases her leg over toward the edge of the bed and whispers, "Yes." It must be midnight or early Wednesday morning.

"Working late," says George. "I'll be over late Thursday."

"All right," says Fiona.

"Some stuff has come up," he adds.

"Oh," says Fiona. . . . Now she can go to sleep, plant the flowers tomorrow, a day to stay home and relax.

" 'Bye now," says George, and makes a kissing noise.

"I'll be waiting," says Fiona. "Good night," she adds, but George has hung up.

Her duties are finished for the day. Sleep, forget, and above all claw out of your mind the picture of that lucky kitten huddled on the back step curled in newspaper. Fiona fumbles the carafe of water to a glass and permits herself two aspirin for sleep.

Tomorrow won't be better. Take command of yourself because it will be both good and bad like all tomorrows, and that is something she will settle for—if only she can count on that much. Her knee throbs. She closes her eyes. No rhyme and no reason to it, quite senseless, the murder of the kitten, but so sensible in a mad, filthy, feuding, ugly world.

9
Wednesday, August 11.

It has been a lovely day. Pristine white pots holding bouffant white petunias line the bookshelves. Beautiful. And Fiona turns on the evening news. She fluffs her hair, freshly washed and still damp.

The Toby Mug star waits in the wings while the introduction is made as full of suspense as possible by the blurbing curtain raiser: "Six o'clock news," a man shouts. "At the top of the news a riot in Watts, right after this message."

Maybe the blacks aren't swallowing so well, or they are having themselves a rest from swallowing . . . and here is the prima donna, the Toby Mug at last, after an extensive ad for cigarettes—a dancing long-haired girl wandering through a field of poppies to join a dancing boy smoking cigarettes. Perhaps Madison Avenue has gone on pot too.

The Toby Mug is slavering all over himself at the hot story he's got, doesn't even have to make it dramatic this time.

Today a highwayman of the law comes happily upon

a speeder, and since a chase is the most exciting thing that can happen to him in long dull hours of shifting gears at stoplights and cruising on and on and ever onward, he gets on to him with a right good will.

He rams the starter down, kicks and thunders the cycle to life, and springs away into the center of the roadway. Hunching over the bars, he hurtles along at the speed of an express train, parting the street traffic as citizens scurry like disturbed ants to get the hell out of a king's path. They idle outranked motors along the curbs as he roars by in command of the road and nails two young black men in their car.

"Out, out," the lawman orders, and the two scramble to comply. And down over the hood, stomachs flat, they are rapped up and down their backsides. Fiona has seen it many times. She can see what the Toby Mug is describing.

No weapons. So far, so good. The drunk test. Today the driver flunks, so the lawman turns to the cycle that is so dramatically equipped with the means to call for immediate help in apprehending the culprits.

The rider must be arrested too, the driver's younger brother. And don't forget to arrest the swine's car as well. The brother suggests he can take the car home for his mother. Don't be so stupid, dummy. The car is arrested too. And you too. And him too, because no one is loggin' off nowhere, buddy boy.

It is nice and hot and steamy in Watts and all the blacks are outside today before their little houses and flats and cubbyholes, sitting on steps, lolling along walls, watching this show, no matter how old and stale and without deviation from the same old thing.

The authorities gather, many lawmen come tearing up

on motorcycles. A tow truck roars into the area. A black and white squad car arrives. Soon the battle will begin.

The driver's ma arrives and scolds her ex-soldier son for boozing. The idlers on step and walk draw near. There is a crowd of three hundred or more in need of diversion.

The soldier son begins to swear and protest his arrest. More help is called to the scene. Three more lawmen arrive in minutes. Mama turns sour on the deal and lashes out at a lawman ripping her son's shirt. A policeman swings at the arrested boy with his night stick, cutting the lad's face. They now arrest Ma, both boys, and the car as more lawmen arrive. Representatives of law and order in massive overreaction by this time include state, country, and city. On the other side are some one thousand blacks looking for diversion.

Authorities make ready to leave the scene in some hurry. A black spits on a lawman. One more black is arrested, not only the spitter but his companion as well.

The last police car to leave the scene is stoned and Watts is on the boil; soon it will boil right over.

Fiona knows the fine feeling these blacks have at heaving stones and chucking bricks. The blacks know well the feeling that Grandpaw has when he chucks stones against the fence of the old shrew whose dogs bark. Fiona knows too.

The Toby Mug is beside himself with delight; he's been given extra time to stay on top of Watts. All the funny, funny little family shows for certain families to enjoy, pale-faces in trim backyards having hamburgers grilled on barbecue installations beside the pool, are swept right off television. Fiona is in for an entertaining evening. She is happy George won't be coming until tomorrow night.

Between eight and midnight Fiona watches mobs stone

cars, yank palefaces out of them, beat them up while the
police set up command posts; then it is announced with
satisfaction that thirty anarchists are safely shut away behind bars. That ought to teach them something.

Fiona takes a little watering can with a long spout and
is carefully sprinkling all the little white pots of petunias
marching along the front of the bookshelves when there is
a news break in the immediate fighting front in Watts to
go to the fighting front in Vietnam.

When aircraft fires five thousand machine-gun bullets
a minute on those below in Vietnam, it's a riot in Watts
multiplied. Over there, those below wait like butterflies
caught at the ends of pins. There's no place to hide, no
escape, no chance to announce, "Say, Mister, I ain't mad at
nobody." Quite useless, because the rain of death is an im-
personal mathematical operation. "And if we don't catch
you this time, there are some new bombs that don't explode
for six months after they're dropped. So who knows when
we'll get you? But get you we will." The scoreboard of
today's dead, the enemy North Vietnamese, two thousand
four hundred, and they don't mention that the dead on
any side include men, women, children, animals, crops,
because even the newscaster isn't so stupid. . . .

Back to Watts news again. See the glazed dumb look on
the faces of the hurt in the hospital. No one speaks. The
camera takes an impartial look at the floor covered in blood.
It's a pity the lens can't reproduce the smell; it must stink
of sweet urine like the dead kitten. No one is alive here,
only dumb and numb. Like a Vietnam divided into many
Wattses. Tonight Watts is part of Vietnam.

Fiona watches a car overturned and burning. She grunts
to help as they heave at another and strain to get it over.

97

The back wheel of a car is spinning in air. A paleface staggers along, his handkerchief held to the side of his face. He leans against a lamppost, dazed, still mopping at it. Fiona has ached to throw a brick through plate glass; she longed many times to wail and kick and scream and be a firebug. Such pleasure she takes in seeing these people with the guts and the "what-have-we-got-to-lose" courage. Take action, that's it. What a fine release they must feel inside. Take that, and that, and that! A punishing, senseless violence, because they can't win. But in the sum of days spent in the continual round of contempt so thinly veiled in the eyes of palefaces, always swallowing down one more spoonful of the bitter medicine to add to the frustration and hurt already brewing inside, always adding more to the cauldron to be sure the fire never burns out; swallowing it down silently, quietly; banking the seething of the old doses still hot with fire—for many, there is fine relief in this uprising.

Haven't I got the low-caste mark branded visibly for all to see? Don't I know I'm marked? Why must I be punished further for an inherited misfortune?

Fiona snaps off the television and prepares for bed. She changes the dressing on her knee. It is healing nicely. George won't notice it tomorrow night. She washes her face with baby soap and rinses it well. She brushes her hair and takes the small radio from a drawer, tunes it to the only thing on the air—the Watts uprising—and prepares to sleep.

Tomorrow she must go to the washhouse; she wants everything nice for George. She will serve the Cold Duck wine with supper. George will like that. As she falls asleep the announcer is shouting, "The Negroes have taken over in Watts! More police are going in! . . ."

98

10
Thursday, August 12.

After changing the bed, Fiona gathers towels, pillow slips, and sheets and stuffs them into the canvas bag. She hopes the place will be deserted, what with the early hour of the day and the riot in Watts still in full swing.

Although dreaded, encounters at the washhouse are seldom hostile, and they are not always with talkative types so intent on themselves as to leave no recognition of Fiona's color. No, mostly these meetings are marked by a studied indifference. Fiona is not there in most cases. She's not even as much as the nuisance of a bug to brush off the collar. No sir, a hiatus of absolute nothing comes down between Fiona and the others. All she need do is manage the polite motions of clearing herself from their area. They are so intent on accomplishing the same purpose, "getting shut of" Fiona and all her ilk, there are few difficulties as a rule. She can't count on this kind of situation today, but she can hope for it.

Perhaps by tonight the rebels in Watts will all be stuffed back secure in their bottles. All corked and shut up. Then, if not shaken, they can be kept capped, at least for a while.

Fiona's radio reports an uneasy calm, but tension running high. A meeting has been called in the park and there is hope for negotiation; talk it all over with reason, announcers say.

At the washhouse Fiona is unpleasantly amazed. There are at least five housewives present. There are two black men who keep stepping aside and backing off to allow paleface customers to be first at soap and bleach machines.

She can see, with this mess in Watts, blacks are behaving more apologetically than usual, in true servile self-effacing manner; they wish to survive the Watts threat too.

Fiona understands their fear. She's fearful most of her life of many things: jail, police, parents, anyone, anything, the works, right now, today, too.

The dried-up, wrinkled, old black woman standing between the rank of driers and the folding table, twisting a towel in her claw hands, has gone a gray color and looks very much like a spider. She is, without any warning, screeching up into the face of a paleface man whose neck is turning beet red in massive rage.

Fiona ducks her head down and takes wet wash from her machine.

"Listen, nigger, I said you'll leave my clothes to hell alone or I'll see you get a free ride back down South where we know how to handle you bastards," says the man.

The old woman is bent almost double. It is her natural skinny shape. Crippled crooked by time and misuse, a born loser, that's her. But, unbelievably, she is shouting back at the man. "Y'all don't git to hell back here and git them clothes out of the drier when they's dry, then we got the right to remove them. Says so on that big sign right up there," she fumes at him, breathing hard. She abuses her

100

lips, biting, chewing, tucking them in and blowing them out. She rocks herself, with her hands on her bony hips, she turns her tiny grizzled head with a small twist of white hair on top right up into his red face.

Such spunk, such unbridled courage, Fiona thinks, wishing she had only a bit of this ridiculously tiny old woman's guts.

Fiona trembles where she stands by an end-of-the-row drier. This is the one placed farthest from the encounter, but not far enough to suit Fiona. Paleface washers gather about the old woman, who appears to play to them as though to a friendly audience. She does not seem to realize they are hostile to her, this old nigger woman turning gray color, a smart aleck who doesn't know any better than to defy and answer back to a white man. Doesn't she know she must never, never, touch an overdried washing belonging to a white man? No matter if she needs a drier for her own wash.

The two stand glaring at each other. The hulk of the man's body appears crouched over the tiny old woman, who looks as though she's been in the drier too, and been shrunken and overdried along with his clothes.

The hot red face of the man turns away first. He tosses his wrinkled clothes into a basket, shoving them from the folding counter where the old woman has piled them. He collects his soap, his bottle of bleach, and turns to go. "I'm warning you, your time's comin', nigger."

Fiona waits, wishing to be part of the dirty pink wall. A cold wind blows about her neck as in Las Vegas; a chill fear grips her, a feeling of foreboding. She sees the group with the old woman and the raging man are moving down near her drier; she will have to wait to get her clothes out.

She moves nearer the bulletin board and pretends an interest in all the curling bits of paper attached to it.

The old woman dances about in agitation, her back is bent, and the black cords in her skinny arms stand out as she collects her clothes and jams them into a hand basket.

The man goes out and slams his car away from the building. The old woman mutters and bobs her head, feinting and ducking in the manner of a spry, punch-drunk fighter with bandy legs who keeps coming up again and again in spite of the sound of a final countdown.

Fiona reads again one of the selections of graffiti also pinned to the board. In an attempt to calm herself, she reads the large black lettering: "SO THEY LAID THE BABY IN THE MANGER AND A COW ATE IT."

Hell! She'll get out of here and back to the sanctuary of her gray cement termite-eaten shelter as soon as possible. She rams her laundry, without folding it, into the bag. The old woman stomps out and all the palefaces laugh like fiends behind her. They double themselves over laughing and make giggling, stifled snorts as they rehash the free and unexpected diversion of it all. One of them tosses an empty bleach bottle at the old woman, but it falls harmlessly to the doorstep behind her.

Through it all Fiona only hopes the police won't be called before she can pull her stuff from the drier and get out. Many people call the police on a thing like this to lengthen it out, drag it on, and further relieve their boredom.

"That's something," Fiona says to herself, safely out of there and walking quickly along the rotting sidewalk, watching her step so she doesn't trip again. "Boredom, wardom, whoredom—my life story in three words."

Why didn't she say a word in defense of the old woman,

who, in spite of the ready back talk, is in fear of her very life with this angry man? One slight twist of her neck, shriveled almost to the small size of the kitten's, is all it would need, and the man was ready to do it too.

Who in that hostile group would tell the truth? Who won't say it was an accident, the old woman hurt herself?

What is more, and worse—even stupid—courageless Fiona will say it is not murder. I saw nothing, she will say. No guts, that is Fiona. And the old woman is right. When driers are filled and some clothes are dry, remove them, even if the owner isn't present. Place them on the counter and take the drier. That's the rule. But not for blacks. Get that through your thick head. Do I say a word to help her? No, I hang by the bulletin board hoping not to be noticed, afraid. And I am a dirty mother of a nothing, as the tar man sings it. Even he knows a coward, and apart from my profession and color, which he knows too.

At home Fiona hangs fresh towels, puts the laundry away, and takes the little radio to the kitchen while she prepares some food. George is coming tonight; someone to talk to, and he will talk to her.

The radio man says a meeting has been held in the park where a young tough black grabs the mike and announces there will be an attack and foray into white neighborhoods tonight. He screams it before they can snatch the mike away from his big mouth, the announcer reports.

Logically, blacks ask that white cops be withdrawn from Watts and black ones put in their place. "Ain't got that many in uniform, thank God," says a cop. The announcer adds a flash: "The Guard will be called."

Oh, George will be thrilled.

Now the announcer says there is a slight hitch to getting

permission to call the Guard. The Governor is in Europe. The Acting Governor can't decide. Meanwhile things are warming up again in Watts. Firemen on trucks are being stoned; their engines are being set on fire; firemen are refusing to go in there at all. Let the fires burn.

Fiona snaps the radio off. She puts the sandwiches, salad, celery, olives, and pickles, wrapped in waxed paper and then in foil, in the refrigerator.

She will have a leisurely bath. She'll wear her smart black jersey nightgown. Its cut makes it lie so close to her figure it is as though her beige color has turned black. There is neat fluting of narrow pleats about the bottom of it, and about the arms and off-the-shoulder neckline too. George will love it and then enjoy stripping it off.

By eleven he has arrived. Fiona opens the wine and without warning the bottle sends its cork with a loud firing report to the ceiling. The wine spews upward in a steady stream while George laughs and rubs himself against Fiona's behind. He says it sounds like the Viet Cong laying in a round of mortars. Most of the wine is now pink across the ceiling. Fiona opens a rosé for their supper. She puts on the record player the marches George prefers, especially Elgar's "Pomp and Circumstance, No. 1," composed for the coronation of Edward VII, a title taken from Shakespeare's "Othello": "Pride, pomp, and circumstance of glorious war."

The Boston Pops sounds out with it as Fiona pours the wine into long-stemmed glasses. George huddles happily down over his sandwiches and winks at Fiona. "Say, I'm ready for you already, Fiona," he comments with anticipating relish.

104

PART FOUR

11
Friday, August 13. 4:00 P.M.

Hasn't the past week been bad enough? No. This one is starting out as though trying to top it! Fiona is still hunching over the coffee table with its curling sandwiches and soiled cups. Maybe Humel will never return. Maybe horses will fly. She stares into the dark screen, willing herself into the sanctuary of its leafy wilderness. I am starting to run like the little wolf. Only where am I to run? There isn't anyplace. How I would adore a man like Martin Luther King. If only I can meet one like him. But he's happily married. Look at the elegance of his wife. But only to creep beneath the protection of a man like that, or the other one King makes her think of, the man of India; Gandhi, that's the one! Other people can have her share of the excitement of war and violence. Oh God, there's no good wishing, no good spending time whining for money to go to movies or for candy, as she remembers doing while yet a stupid child.

Better get busy; go to the store, which she ought to have done on the way back from the washhouse, because now in the afternoon it is hot—hot in more ways than one. She must have supplies for the new man. Must have a new man. How long will her small capital last if she's forced on the run like the hounded, wretched animal? I now command myself to forget that wolf.

Let's see. I have liquor. He will run to Scotch and soda. I need soda. And ham for sandwiches; maybe a sweet. They are always on a diet but can't resist my pie after I show it to them. I ought to make a pie, but it's so hot and there isn't much time. Almost five and I ought to leave here by seven at the latest. It will take time to prepare the supper too.

Fiona is up and clearing the coffee table. She fluffs the pillows, brushes the cushions. She takes her purse and moves out of the house, unlocks the gate and out to the court. Now she is on the filthy, smeared paving of it again. The obscene odors in the stifling air assails her nostrils. Ear-splitting noises assault her as well. She glances away quickly from the wormy plants along the edges of the melting tar of the center paving. The insect life swarms: fleas, mites, aphids, flies, and, most of all, worms. She passes a house with a striped circus tent over it. In there they are trying to poison some of the cockroaches with a cynanide treatment. So futile! The eggs in the walls will survive and the old house will run with them again. The death tent for insects covers many houses in the area over and over again.

An old man is approaching; he creeps closer to her in a bent-over, slowly stooping walk. He passes her, head down, looking at cracks in the paving and studying them intently.

109

Now the roar and clang and din of trucks, buses, and cars come closer to her and she waits at the curb of the boulevard for the lights to change. The cars pant and huff near her legs as she steps out to cross before them. The bumpers quiver and pulse to get her to hell out of the way for their next charging run; the beat of the motors sound with her heartbeats. She reaches the opposite side, but the old shoemaker has not been so lucky. He was killed last Friday, the grocery man tells her, just stepping across from his shop to buy a Coke.

She picks up fresh rye bread, sweet butter, lettuce, Danish ham, and a bottle of soda. "Bye," she says to the groceryman. "Have a nice weekend," he answers as she picks up the large sack.

Quickly she returns along all these worlds within more worlds of the Court; the muted sounds of the decaying dead and dying drum in her mind with her steps. Shall I meet a violent end like the shoe man? If so, I won't be able to do a thing about it. This sudden knowledge snaps into her mind like a street lamp springing to life. Arrested and alert at this electric thought, she skirts a dog trotting by, as though he may be the means of this bad finish. She flicks her head to rid herself of these foul thoughts and tells herself to hurry up, get home, and dress to leave for the hotel, where she can get in touch with George. She dare not call him now. The corporation is locked up for the weekend anyway; besides, he is happy in uniform, helping to put down a riot.

At last she sits at the dressing table planning her own décor for the evening. She brushes her hair. At least that was a break. Plenty of body, as they say; thick and only slightly curly. Once a week baby oil, then baby shampoo; allow it to dry, brush; place large curlers, turned up, about the ends, then brush again and it's ready.

Thursday is the day for it, just in case she must make an unscheduled Friday-night appearance at the Mar Vista in search of the next company. But this week, after what Las Vegas did to it, she is forced to take care of it Wednesday. Still, it gleams and looks lovely. She applies baby hand lotion to her face. Cosmetics aren't for black skin. Looks like clown makeup. But she knows what to use. Only bronze eye shadow, and a lipstick the color of the inside of her lips, a petal-pale pink. For the rest, French oil and lots of Castile baby soap, and many rinsings. She strokes her cheek in appreciation of the clear, fine-pored skin; no blotches, freckles, or pimples mar its surface. Her eyebrows are neat and arched, and now for the long bath with plenty of oils and perfumes.

She lies back in the scented water. Why worry? There will be nothing to it. Of course she'll tell Humel she will be happy to go on seeing George. When George finds out about her troubles, he'll help her. But she must get the message to him, or Humel can ruin her careful years of anonymity.

Tonight she'll wear the fine black wool with its delicate trim of barely visible black braid etched along the round neck and about the short sleeves. The flat gold pin at her waist, a wide rectangle with cutwork interior of a narrow road running far away over a hill into a descending sun. She likes it. Oh, yes; on her marriage finger the heavily carved scarab ring of gold with its center glowing of black pearl, surrounded by lacy rope of more gold.

Why didn't she realize Humel wants far more from her than talk? Still, she can credit herself with the fact that today she suspects him.

She has nice hands. She lifts them from the water and plunges them back again, liking the look of them fluffed about with curls and beads of white soapy bubbles. They look almost white with this thin glaze of soap and water. She nods her head at herself in the sunburst mirror of Mexican silver at the foot of the tub. She decorates her shoulders with plumes and sprays of soapsuds and reminds herself of a very old ivory treasure, a figurine nicely smoked with nicotine. She cocks her head in an arrogant tilt and smiles at herself. Dentists deplore the nicotined look of teeth, and they diligently scrape and pick and bleach until teeth are snow white again. Pity there is nothing they can do about skin, prized as treasure only when the color remains on ivory figurines; otherwise the color is black.

She'll wear the black raincoat tonight over her dress. It is light and yet provides cover to help blend herself into twilight-gray streets. There will probably be smog, and the fog drifting in from the sea. All the fires burning in Watts are blowing a smudge in this direction too.

She'll be safe in a taxi. She never goes on foot into the loose ash-blowing, dingy streets at night anyway. This is the way to come to the attention of the law in southern California. No one—even white and with impeccable credentials about his person—walks streets at night unless he doesn't mind being examined by the police.

Who will she meet tonight? Will her kind be there? Of course, they always are, politically Republicans, religiously Christians, university-educated, clothed in shiny dark suits. They have waists too wide, and necks too short, and heads too cropped, and watches too thin, and billfolds smelling of new leather, and French cuffs with silver rather than gold links. They will drink Scotch, Cutty Sark, and will like best a girl with a joyous attitude, who can wear clothes well. (There is a certain cachet about a high-status black girl.) They shave often, brush teeth more than necessary, visit dentist regularly, and now and then smoke a cigar, but mostly cigarettes with charcoal filters; they wear shorts to bed and Tee shirts rarely.

He will be there tonight because it's club night. "Thank-God-it's-Friday" night, so he'll be at the Mar Vista, the cheap-looking hotel for all the expense of its fat-stomached gargoyles, slitty-eyed masks, brushy plants, and waiters wearing sloppy Hawaiian shirts.

When she says good-by to George, why doesn't she say, "Thank you very much, George, I had a nice time," because isn't that the story of her life in many ways? It's a lie, of course, because she hasn't had a very nice time at all. But what can she do about it now except conspire to survive?

In a long white dressing gown and white-beaded Indian slippers, Fiona turns on the television. The Friday newsman, not the Toby Mug, is the confused one. It always entertains her to see him fumble among his slips of paper for the one he searches for and can't find, meanwhile going right along talking, talking. Frantically he continues his quest for the bit that always escapes him. He makes false starts, he mumbles, and offers several excuse me's. Oh, he's a mixed-up mess of nonsense and makes Fiona laugh out loud. Suddenly he sits erect like a bird dog on point. He's alert and on the qui vive as he barks out that police are more than doing their duty in Watts. Whitey's bodyguards, why not? she is thinking. He says they are being shot at by this pigmented bunch. Well, blacks aren't represented by the dressed-up-in-black-and-white policemen anyway. Their black boots are treading along before the palaces of authority all over the world, marching to law and order, not right and left. I'd say they are a big flop at the job too. What have they maintained by way of law and order?

The announcer is outraged at this failure of maximum security. He talks about pushy Negroes and he is clever, this mixed-up one; he does not make statements. He asks his points, makes questions of them. Don't you agree this, and don't you think that? The man casts aside all his slips of paper for a real heart-to-heart with the good citizens out there. Fiona knows the pushy types he talks about; "liberals," he all but spits out; these people Hitler hates; this man does too. Oh, to hell with this oaf, and she snaps him off.

Prepare yourself for your job. You are one with those who live in the primitive days when sex is a sacred duty. The princesses, and slaves too, prostitute themselves for spiritual salvation. That is what I am doing, saving myself.

Fiona bends over the hand mirror at the dressing table. This is what I shall be like when I'm old. Her face sags into a wrinkled map of the old woman in the washhouse. No—she slaps the mirror back to the top of the table and sits very straight, staring at herself in the glass—not yet. She picks up the spray cologne, her favorite Joyous Heart—a delicate scent of spring violets, peonies after rain, that kind of perfume—and she sprays herself head to foot. In a cloud of this she moves to the bed and sprays that liberally as well, dollars' and dollars' worth of scented delight under the pillows, between the sheets, over the spread. Now she

114

walks in springtime through a meadow solidly packed with nosegays: "Coeur-joie."

She sits at her desk and draws out a piece of thick white paper. She picks up a silver pen, dips it into black ink, and in a finishing-school, erect, angular script writes: "Leave number with Jack. I must call you soonest! Imperative I speak to you!"

She takes another sheet and practices a long line of ovals; elegant spirals, over and over, decorate the paper. She makes a ball of that, tosses it into the basket, and writes a large capital F at the end of the note to George. She blots the initial, folds and places the square into the white envelope. She inscribes it with G. Aiken and puts it into her black handbag that is handmade by Fiona, gathered in narrow pleats into a silver frame. She admires it, smoothing it with her hand.

It is time to go. She takes out the raincoat and removes the money from the pocket. She puts that into her purse too. She may need money to buy her way through some difficulty. The raincoat whispers and clicks about her bare wrists. She ties the belt and takes a last look at her dusky image. She looks very smart. She calls a taxi and stands by the back door waiting for it. When the horn sounds, she locks the back door. All the lights are out, so she picks her way slowly to the gate. She has an inclination to hold her nose against the scents of the Court.

"Where to?" the man asks.

"Mar Vista, please."

The driver makes the boulevard in one racing lunge, braking sharply. Fiona holds on to the handle beneath the window and braces herself with toes against the back of the front seat. The white driver knows she's black.

The boulevard sidewalks are deserted; uncanny, the way traffic has died. It's a day town. At night people leave the area. A cruising squad car passes by, going slowly. Friday-night shoppers, safely encased in their automobiles, also pass along, their destination the weekend carnival of shopping centers. The man of the family will soon be parted from much of his paycheck just received. Groceries, shoes, dresses, a new television, and now a gun, too, are on many lists. The people are not staying home as they have been asked to do until the riot is put down.

Within a block of the entrance to the hotel, Fiona asks to get out of the cab. Her tough old Cockney friend, who has drifted somehow to Santa Monica, stands by her newspaper corner. Fiona must say hello.

The woman slaps at her dirty skirt with a rolled-up paper.

Fiona pays the man and he snorts the car away fast, his radio blaring riot news.

The tacky old woman with her horrible accent is not permitted to sell papers inside the splendor of the lobby of the Mar Vista, so she sits on a little stool at her stand, a block from it. Born within the sound of Bow Bells in London, some sixty years before, she tells Fiona the queen is a Cockney too. She doesn't seem to mind the color of Fiona's skin, perhaps because her own appearance includes a leather-looking hat stiff with dirt, and she wears it straight on, pulling a few sprigs of wiry, bent gray hair into chopped whisk-broom clumps to stick out on either side of her leathery brown face. The skin is not only burned dark but heavily furrowed too, and one eye hangs in a cast that gives her the wicked look of an old rip. She tells Fiona that what she can see with the eye she's got left makes her sick enough to be happy she can't see with two.

116

One day she tells Fiona how sick these young girls make her; ignorant tramps, the lot of them, she says. She'd like to slap them about the "fice," she says. One winter she damned near dies and would have, too, if she'd stopped another day in the bloody 'ospital they'd carted her off to. When the young nurses turned their silly backs, she put on her leather hat and coat and cleared off.

"Blimey, if it ain't our girl! 'Ow are yer?" the old woman greets her.

"Hi, how are you?" Fiona says.

The old woman sips at a tin cup of stout, her favorite drink for her long hours of standing and yelling headlines now and again. "Better get out of 'ere, dearie, while you may. It ain't no place for you, me girl," she advises Fiona.

"Do you think it my fate to die here?" Fiona asks.

"Wot's the difference? We're all alike. If yer won't be hung, you'll be drown. A matter of time," and the old woman slaps at her leg with a paper.

"How is your daughter and her family?" Fiona asks.

"Well, she calls me down to Long Beach not but a week ago. Give up me job here. For what? Tike care of 'er just home from 'ospital. Wot a devil the cheeky daughter is, bit of a kid, sixteen. Give me lip, she did. Shouted at me, she did. Wasn't going to do this or that and so on. 'Oh gor blind me,' I shouted back at 'er. 'Yer gives me any more of yer lip and I'll lay me fist to 'yer bloody chops, I will, ain't got a brass ear 'ole,' I says to 'er. There'll be a radical change with that bird before I go round there again and offer me services I can tell yer, I choked 'er off proper."

"I must go," says Fiona. "See you later."

"Tike care of yerself, me girl: don't look good in the lights."

"I will," says Fiona.

"Bye-bye, dearie. Say, will yer ask that boy to send me down another jar of stout, there's a good girl."

"Sure. 'Bye," says Fiona and walks down the block to the front entrance that faces the sea. She crosses the carpet stretching to the curb, tips a bellhop in the lobby to send her friend the drink. She relishes the chance to do this favor for a friend. It is good to have a friend to do a favor for—so soothing, so normal.

12
Friday, August 13. 7:00 P.M.

Fiona stands at the entrance to the Island Room. The headwaiter asks, "For one? Dinner?"

"Yes, please, dinner. I shall be joined later," she says.

She follows him.

"The table there in the corner, please," she says.

"Fine," he says, admiring her, and pulls out the table so she can slip behind it.

"May I take your coat?"

"No thanks, I'll just slip it off here."

She orders a drink, the specialité, a pineapple shell filled with rum and fruit juices and God knows what. She will sip it for hours if need be. That's it for the evening when she buys. Hopefully, she may get this one paid for. A matter of time. Time is of the essence. She watches the room fill up with the chortling, her kind of corporation men. They are dotted about at tables in the center of the room, or they sit along the leather banquettes at the edges, among giant statues and tall trees and bushes. The lights are amber and very low.

Fiona is accustomed to George's smell. His known scent smells secure to her. The alien smell of the new man is not exciting to contemplate; it is a fearsome thing. What will the new man smell like, his unique-to-himself smell?

"Will you please give this note to Jack?" she asks her waiter.

"Of course," he says, placing the tall pineapple drink on a tiny napkin and moving the ashtray near her elbow.

"Would you like to order dinner now?" he asks.

"No thanks, later."

"Certainly."

She watches as he approaches Jack, who nods at her and puts the note beside the cash register at the back of the bar. He serves another tired executive. His third Scotch, Fiona counts, although the other two drinks do not look finished; they stand beside the fresh one Jack places before him. A peculiar type, no doubt, but harmless. The man is alone. He looks at her and away again. He is cut to the pattern—suit, hair, age; thirty-five perhaps, and bored. The waiter comes to her again. "The gentleman at the bar wishes to know if he may join you?"

"Yes," says Fiona.

Promptly he comes to her table, bringing only his last drink and his cigarettes.

"Hello," he says. "Thanks for letting me join you. Appreciate it. Frankly, I'm bored. My name's John. What's yours?"

"Fiona James," she says.

"Is someone coming to join you?"

"I'm not sure. I'm waiting for a phone call, but if I'm not here, I've left a note," she says.

"I watched you come in. Such grace. Are you a dancer?"

"No. Sorry."

"I don't mind. I understand they're usually tired—on oxygen, like my wife, as a matter of fact."

"Is your wife a dancer?"

"She's too tired for everything, not to mention dancing."

"Sorry."

"I've got her picture here; doesn't look so tired." He pulls out the thin leather billfold, flips the cellophane laminated pages. "There you are."

"Very attractive," says Fiona. She sees at a glance the wife has the martyred look, for all the brave smile. Why are men so emotional before marriage when women are calculating, and after marriage the roles are reversed? She can see the wife is inclined to be a weeper; her eyes squint and her features, even touched up by the photographer, show a woman ready to weep at any moment.

"Here are the three kids," he says, pointing to a girl and two boys clinging close to one another at the edge of a swimming pool, clutching as though in early alliance for mutual advantage.

"It must be a job keeping up with those healthy specimens," says Fiona gallantly, gazing at the nervous-looking arms entwined about each other.

"No, she has a nurse for the two youngest—from England,

as a matter of fact. She lives in, goes to the university at night. The older boy is away at boarding school now; comes home only on holidays."

"I see. But still, it must be quite a responsibility," says Fiona, hoping he will soon put away the entire misalliance and get on with the business at hand. His mucking along at such length with these preliminaries makes her think of the endless time ahead for him when, in old age, he'll have to slow to a crawl. She can mark in his face, and in that photo of his wife, that in those old-age years the kids will begin the lusty fight over whose responsibility it is to care for these incapacitated ancient parents.

Say she dies first, so they can't cling together for comfort in misery any more; the one left alone will find a lousy helpless old age stretching before him. There won't be enough money; never is; so these three will hold nasty, secretive, behind-his-back councils of war. Battle lines will be drawn by the grown children. They will discuss endlessly the old man, and tear to shreds the last of his dignity and privacy. They will stage an invasion of their own blood. What to do with this problem? When they themselves were young, they were the problem; the parents worried. Now the burden is reversed, "Such a financial drain," they will chime. "I mean, all his medicine alone, and special foods too," and he becomes the source of griping care and worry.

Now a young man sits beside her, but soon he will be the old man. Right now he is removed from his children's squabbling, but when he's old, it will reach his ears—it always does—where it will sear and burn, this knowledge of rejection, the helpless, poor old devil. "What's it all about?" he will ask himself then. Christ, buddy! Do what you can now, buddy, because it will come to you. The tranquil-old-age stuff is a myth, a dream that won't come true. Like me, you'll be alone, and it will be easier for me among strangers who will let me have it right to my face, then and now.

"I was wondering if you'll be free any time this evening? Will you have dinner with me and go dancing later?"

"Thanks, I'll have to see."

"Actually, I was asked to sit with those fellows over there at that table," he is saying, "but I see them all week and I'm sick of them."

"They seem to be having a fine time."

"The one over there on the left got a raise. Another million-dollar-or-so contract at Space Unlimited. That one helped negotiate it," he says, and Fiona realizes this is George's corporation.

"They are all safely married, I guess."

"No, that one beside him is free, white and——" He stops and sips his drink. "Sorry. Actually, I believe in the Negro revolution. May I be candid about it?"

"Why not? And I'm black, over twenty-one, and far from free."

"Are you married?"

There are other ways besides skin color and marriage to become a captive, she is thinking. "I'm not married," she says.

"What do you do in your spare time?"

"Besides my main line, entertaining one man at a time and often for a year or more at a time, I like to work in the garden, but I haven't been able to do much of that in this last place."

She wants to say, "Don't dare hang outside that long, might stir up complaints," but she refrains. Bitterness won't

122

make it with him or most men, for that matter. The cement private house is still better than an apartment; at least she can look at the garden.

"Are you free now? I mean, with the entertaining bit?"

"Yes."

"Where do you live?"

"I have a house in Venice; rather a nice one too."

"There's a call for you, Miss James. Jack says you can take it at the bar if you want," says the waiter.

"Oh, thanks. . . . Excuse me, John."

He gets up and pulls back the table for Fiona.

George sounds out of his mind with excitement. He is out of breath and panting. "Yes, Fiona, it's me. I called here on the chance you'd be there."

"Thank God, George. Listen, give me a number where I can reach you. I can't talk here at the bar. I can call you when I get home."

"Listen, you shouldn't go there tonight—my wife—that's why I wanted to reach you."

"I'll have someone with me; he can answer the door."

"Already, huh?"

"Listen, George, I've got to talk to you about something extremely important. Give me a number. He'll be out of the room, in the bath or something, and I'll call you."

"Okay, I'm at Guard Headquarters here. If you can't get me by ten o'clock, I'll call you at the house."

"Be careful, George. I'm glad you are where you are."

"What's that supposed to mean?"

"You're safer there."

"Is this some kind of joke?"

"I'll explain later. 'Bye. Have to go."

"Okay." George hangs up.

"About my gardening . . ." Fiona begins, back at the table.

"Will you be joined by your date, or is it my night?" John asks.

"It's your night, and I take it you are not too interested in gardens."

"I'm more interested in you. Shall we have another drink and then order dinner?"

"Fine."

In the taxi on the way back to the house, Fiona plans to serve drinks in the bedroom and, after John is nicely taken care of—and no rushing—she will call George. Two more drinks for John, and sex too, will see him in a relaxed snoring mood. All lights out in case George's wife shows up this late, and then call George.

In the taxi John holds her hand and kisses her, to the disgust of the driver, another paleface. The boulevard is quiet except for squad cars moving along at a crawl and flashing spotlights into courts and alleys.

They drive to the back gate and stop. John pays the man and she precedes him to find the keys and open the door. Inside she puts on only the tiny light over the stove and leads the way to the sitting room, where she turns on one small lamp by the wing chair. "Will you have a drink?" she asks.

He hands her a leather case. Not pictures again! Not a man with a conscience she'll need to soothe and put up with! Still, a first time for everything, and she opens the case to a gold seal. She feels weak about the knees, as though she's spent hours in bed with George.

"Yes, I'm a Federal agent. Sorry to fool you," he says in

cold sober tones and anything but sorry about it. "I'll only bother you for a moment. We're interested in Humel. We want you to continue with Humel and to go on with your client, Aiken, too. If you refuse, we'll bring you in on several counts: loitering, vagrancy, prostitution, the works. Here's a number where you can call and leave your name, Fiona. Then I'll get back to you. We've got almost everything we want on Humel, but we'd like more. And we want George Aiken to keep on with his same associations, especially you. We count on you to make it possible."

"I see," says Fiona.

"Good night. We'll be around."

She says nothing. John lets himself out the back door.

Now I'm a cornered rat in a trap for sure, a trap I work hours to make soft and padded. So I won't mind being trapped? Like hell I don't. Isn't it enough I'm a whore and a black? No, this is not enough; I'm a cornered rat too.

So the man in Vegas is one of John's pals, making sure George doesn't see Humel. George is directed to take poor sucker Fiona along as camouflage to make his presence there look just like another sexy weekend for Humel's benefit. Is this it? She hopes George croaks. If I'm taken to Vegas as some kind of cover, then George is up to God knows what, a weekend ordered and directed by John, and watched. George isn't above anything; he's a "me-first" survival man; anyone in his way is a minus nothing.

Can I use Watts as a temporary cover for me? But in these present rioting circumstances I may well be slain. Still in this white and pale yellow spying community I may well be knocked off too, or even tortured. Oh, God knows what! Arrested! Not in any case to know the reason why. Except then I won't care. Dead like the little wolf, dead like the

125

little kitten. Of what good my years spent at my clever balancing act for simple survival? Where did I make the bad performance leading to my finish? It's a losing sweet mess. I'm framed, as the hoods say, and a scapegoat for certain.

What is it like to be dead? I can't imagine it, not even the act of dying; can't imagine that either, my breathing body stony still, all juices stopped. What am I going to do? Seven mad days in August since Saturday. Too bad I'm not born a dog. A hippity, hoppity dog, tailing it down the street, up the court, around the town, dodging the odd rock and ignoring the shouts of "Git outta here." I'm discovered, recorded, and singled out for attention by top authorities in the business, so I might as well give up now.

13
Friday, August 13. 11:00 P.M.

Fiona huddles on the bed, rocking herself, knees bound to chin by tightly clasped and rigid arms. She stares out the window at the garden, shrouded in fantastic shapes made up of the botanical killers thriving out there among the plantings. She counts up the oleander, two poinsettia bushes, an elephant ear, a castor-bean tree with leaves broad

126

as tea trays; larkspur; lily of the valley, foxglove, bleeding heart, daphne, wisteria vine; several clumps of laurel, three rhododendron bushes, azaleas along the ivy-covered fence, jasmine, a yew tree, a wild-cherry tree, a black locust, and moonseed, hemlock, deadly nightshade. Oh, she's made a thorough study of them all.

And they are, one and all, deadly poison, the books tell her; either their leaves, berries, or stems; even the roots of some are poison. She loves gardening, just reading about plants. What a fine ecologist she will make if she isn't a cornered rat. She ought to have a farm. Say, she is suddenly a millionaire and buys a few feet of the ex-orange-grove property to be found in California, which is so expensive it is sold by the foot in many places. But really she is good at it. She can make it pay. Certainly she can, but how can she get it?

How about other killers out there—say George's wife lurking along the sidewalk beyond the ivy fence with her adorable gun she's bought for her personal uprising against Fiona?

Oh, I—me—this girl Fiona ought to murder George. He is the one responsible for getting me involved with these spies. I'll be smart to wipe him out. He's the most dangerous person a whore can be mixed up with. I mean, for God's sake, what do I know about George's work? Nothing! Yet me, stupid Fiona, careful as I've been, am suddenly in a trap lined with guns all pointing at me.

Life is two people running. The first one is tossing chairs and dragging tables into the path of the second person pelting along behind in the chase. The second one is continually tripping, falling, and hurting herself. Fiona is the second, chasing a livelihood, and now she's placed in the role of the first, and she must run hard and fast and be certain to leave many obstacles behind her in the way of all those coming along trying to catch her.

If only she can be an old, old lady, whose main concern is just when she may fall victim to cancer of the throat. Yes, there's a tender spot on the left. She feels it, urging and prodding it to respond. She is sometimes conscious of it when she swallows, especially with a dry mouth, such as now.

Perhaps she will linger on in terrible pain after several useless operations, and God, maybe pronounced cured after the insertion of one of those mechanical speaking boxes. Her voice will come out in a tinny squeak and squeal, sounding like metal scratching against metal and attracting attention to her for miles around.

She might be torn apart by dogs, or set upon by night-roving gangs equipped with knives, or torn and raped by a madman. She shakes her head to clear away the fearful images.

And immediately thinks of animals living wild in the forests, coming to violent tragic ends without even interference from the worst enemy, man. They starve to death slowly, or freeze and fall sick and linger; or they are murdered and eaten by larger animals, and sometimes blinded and dash themselves to pieces over cliffs far below. Will she be paid out for her depraved life by several bouts of surgery on the vagina and the big C again, and end with tubes in either nostril pumping air and vitamins and, God, maybe the placing of a cobalt capsule to make her last room smell of cooking meat?

With some luck, she may be knocked senseless by a car like the poor shoemaker. Will she know such a stroke of happy fortune? The death looks good. She's too young for the last killing illness, so all she can look forward to is the luck of sudden death on the boulevard. What can she do meanwhile?

I can call George and then prepare to run fast. Where? If only I can creep into the not-for-real scene on the dead television. But that is out, so where can I run in reality?

If I divide the world into four sections, I will find in the Southwest and Africa plenty of dark skin. In the Southeast, among Australians I will find some more. In Asia, among the Mongolians, there is more dark skin, but I am stuck in the Northwest among light skin. Sure there are pockets like Watts, but comparatively speaking, that is it for the Northwest.

Shall I cross over?

Shall I go into a black ghetto, a short journey compared to going halfway around the world in search of sanctuary? Watts is close by taxi; traffic permitting, perhaps an hour away. A black taxi driver? I can find one to take me inside the lines in Watts where Whitey is persona non grata; Whitey might be murdered with ease.

George's wife is white; the agent is white; and Humel is far from black, a sort of light cream tinged with pale yellow. These three cannot follow me to Watts. It will be a gigantic chair to throw into their paths. George is the crux of it all. Why did I pay the least attention to him when I met him? How could I know then? . . . I must call him.

"Colonel Aiken, please," she says to the snappy fresh-voiced soldier who announces "Guard Headquarters."

Then George is shouting at her, "Hello, hello. . . . Yeah, Fiona," he goes on, keyed up and charged with happiness, brimming over with the joy of war. "What is it?" he raps out, prompting her like a volley of shot.

"George, listen, the sociologist turns out to be a spy."

"Don't be silly, Fiona. I'm plenty busy here. If so, so what? What do you think I can do about it—if interested, which I'm not."

"George, I'm not joking. More important, he isn't joking either. He wants information from you."

"So what? He'll have to want on. My wife already knows about you and I. Forget it."

"There is something else, George. There is a Federal agent involved too. I met him tonight, or I should say he picked me up, introduced himself to me at the hotel."

"Oh! . . . Well, I suggest you make tracks; get out of there. Something else; my mad wife has signed a complaint of some kind; there's a warrant out for you, but you've got time; all the cops are busy here in Watts. Simply pack a grip and find a hotel. Watch out for the boys in the black and white cars on your way. Can't help spotting them ahead of time; never saw so many black and white boys around," says George, still in a blind fever of excitement.

"Okay, George." She only partially dislikes him, really. She has little feeling at all about him, a perfect frame of mind and mood not to care if he lives or dies.

"Yeah, better leave town till the heat's off, as the cons say. I'll straighten out the Chink. The office can take care of the agent. Maybe then I can get down to saving part of this country from rebels down here," George says, his voice thick with self-righteousness.

"George, there's no way for me to get out of town. There's a law against hitching on Los Angeles' freeways. There's too much of a chance to get picked up anywhere tonight. The radio says stay home. I doubt if I can even leave this house without being stopped. What taxi driver wants to take people like me anyplace tonight?"

George doesn't care. He knows she's trapped.

"Oh, hell, Fiona, work it out. I got to go. Get to a hotel someplace—Beverly Hills, Hollywood, someplace."

"Thanks, George." She still has little feeling about him, even if a sniper gets him; very likely, if he is assigned to his troops, a shot in the back. Even so, George is redeemed in death as a tragic hero who put down the blacks.

14
Friday, August 13. MIDNIGHT

Think, Fiona orders herself. Soon it will be tomorrow, Saturday, and early in the morning, down the court will come the big truck to scoop up the garbage spilling over from cans and boxes all along the way. Two blackfaces man the truck. They will be happy to take money to send another blackface in a taxi tonight to get me out of here and into the riot area. George is right. The black-and-whites are too busy to come for me and—who knows?—I may have at least a chance of getting out of this trap where I'm a sitting duck and a fall guy for all of them.

Even the criminals are bewildered. Where is the fuzz? The streets are becoming bare of cops. The confused newsman only last night managed to say that one hundred more policemen, booted, helmeted, night-sticked, and loaded down with guns and ammunition, have been sent into the area.

Yes, now she has a plan. She will lock the house and if they break in with a warrant, they will find her gone; and so will Humel and John. One small suitcase, dark street clothing, the black pants, a black sweater and no beige overjerkin, the black scarf and the raincoat, only a spook face showing, a real nig.

Only a few hours from now she will be able to talk to the garbagemen. She'll go to bed, but she is too excited to sleep, just thinking she may escape. She ought to have thought of this long before and spared herself some harrowing hours. It can be an answer to many of her problems, even those to come. She can find a life for herself among her own kind. The garbageman might even be single; maybe he will marry her; crazier things have happened before. She can live in colored town. After the riot is over, it will sink back to the very same old life and ways. She can go to a black church and meet an honorable citizen of some kind if there is no luck with the garbageman. Maybe this citizen won't mind if his bride has a seamy past. If he won't marry her, then she will offer to live with him for board and room. Someday she might even be entitled to a pension with her new married name, and she can become one of the nutty old women who pick mites from their heads, and who sleep with long-haired, tangled cats inclined to sores on their backs, and lame hind legs. These old ladies are often to be seen carrying a tote bag filled with bits and pieces wherever they go.

Fiona, in spite of nerves strung so high, charging her with the necessity to stay awake and on guard, falls into a troubled nervous, twitching doze. She flinches away from her light dreaming with much distortion of facial expression. Suddenly she is wide awake again, and half sick remembering, too vividly, the sick misery of the time in Europe.

One more time she's made the mistake of falling in love. Wise up. Why waste it? Sell it, don't give it away; it's a commodity and a service and a real need. It's a better mousetrap, fool, and even now, as they did then, tears leak from beneath her lashes, remembering. Before she gets sick and he gives her the go-by, she's trailed him about Europe. Afterward she rarely gives a thought to the lack of splendor in the life she leads when he leaves her. Gin helps; uncombed, unwashed, un-made-up, in the same old dressing gown, she spends a week alone in a boardinghouse. She only looks miserable to others; for herself, there is only pure misery in the life she leads with him before, and she is cold sober then. Never can I, Fiona, rise above the belt with any man. Love's meaning for men is an ode to crotch; and this man is dedicated to nothing else and has the money to finance it. No interference does he brook when it comes to pursuit of the crotch. For Fiona there won't be any marriage with him; what is worse, no love.

Until tonight, it's the worst night of her life. She lay there shivering then just as she does tonight; she is half sick listening for the sound of garbage trucks; then it was to milk wagons creaking by, clop-clopping horses drawing them along over cobbled pavement, and it's early morning too, with a gray light creeping beneath the window blinds. She thinks of prepositions, the way she learns them; think of a sofa, says the teacher; only she thinks of crotch, the same thing; on it, under it, near it, beneath it, to it, round it, for it, by it, of it, between it, in it, over it, at it—a long ode to the crotch for Fiona; a man she loves has one meaning for his life, titillation of crotch. All the pornographic singers and dancers, wearing gaudy costumes and plastered-about face and body with make-up, their suggestive movements flopping about to thumping music, teasing the half-stoned audience sitting out there in the darkness staring at the cavortings of the girls in the spotlight, these are what she drags after him to see, European night clubs that stay in business through the motivation, the stimulation and furthering of the avid interest in preoccupation with the crotch. Handy wipes on fancy cosmetic bars in elegant shops have been replaced with scented spray cans of crotch perfume. Entertainment establishments figure profit and longevity on the staying power of the patron's crotch.

Fiona rolls her head to and fro like a haunted thing, knowing there's nothing else anywhere. All the presents, furs, money, cars, homes, apartments are presented, dedicated, earned, and sweated over to insure nurture and care of the crotch. It's the sum total of all roads, paths expressly laid out to lead below the belt. There is nothing except this in all the world. People work to build a gorgeous crotch house and equip it with a bed. The rest of the structure—kitchen, sitting room, music room, nursery, gardens, library—are nothing but lean-to shacks slapped against the main place of worship, the crotch. The superposition of the crotch main house is the best, the most desired, fought-over damned thing in the whole world.

Fiona twists and turns to escape a fever, an ache and a loss, and even now, as she did then, she listens for the sound of wheels. Can she make it out of the present trap, just as she did then? Yes. She will do the same thing now.

PART
FIVE

15
Saturday, August 14. 5:00 A.M.

Fiona leaves her bed and begins to dress. In the kitchen she can see streaks of light showing up in the east in spite of the competing glow of fires burning down Watts. She puts the teakettle on to heat water for the coffee dripolater. She measures coffee and clears the kitchen neatly. She waters the orange geranium and polishes the copper sugar and creamer used by the traitor, Humel, only yesterday afternoon.

After the tea and watercress sandwiches she's taken such pains to prepare, she is reduced in minutes to making plans for escape to manage bare survival.

She sips coffee and smokes cigarettes and listens for the clamoring hard grind of the truck to come down the Court. One thing, she doesn't wish to be a small child again, young, innocent, carefree, because it isn't like this for Fiona at all.

138

Hanging back by the fence during recess while the class plays the endless game of castle: this is grade school. One day she asks if she can be the maid to the youngest princess. They tell her firmly, "No." In the sixth grade a particularly snotty classmate hits her over the head with a heavy load of books after school one day, and tears spring to her eyes at the shocking pain of the blow.

"Why did you do that?" she asks.

"Because I wanted to," the girl answers.

In junior high, there's a teen-age dance and she borrows from a neighbor a black velvet dress with white lace collar and cuffs. When the husband finds out, he is angry and tells his wife to get the dress cleaned. And she has been so very careful of it.

In high school she wishes to have clothes that match those of classmates, but there isn't any money. She spends long hours using cream, lemon, buttermilk, anything she can think of or read about, to lighten the skin on her face and hands. None of them works; they only make her skin sore. Sometimes at night she considers dipping herself in laundry bleach to see if that might help, but she lacks the courage for it.

At sixteen she knows about prostitutes and even considers such a profession for herself after the incident of the first boy friend, a paleface. After this lesson she figures there's not much else for her to consider. She does not blame her mother. Fiona, the first child, is a perpetual reminder to her mother of her young and stupid days, before she knows where babies come from and not how to prevent having them. She pities her mother.

Fiona tastes power when a paleface classmate gives her lots of attention. But his parents take a dim view of it and

139

are, in fact, so frightened by the childish attachment that they mortgage their home and send the boy away to school, from which he returns only at Christmas and Easter.

But before the parents get the loan to send the boy away, young, ignorant, and silly Fiona asks him home so he can see how light-colored and paleface her family is. She has only one thing on her mind—color.

That afternoon Fiona presses the doorbell sunk into a bed of paint at the side of the gnawed-looking front door. Her paleface boy friend jumps when a thunderous burring emphasis of the ring caused by bad wiring echoes through the overheated television inside.

He jerks his head in apprehension, and Fiona hears her stepgrandmother's voice yelling, "See who the hell is ringing that bell and wrecking my program."

The door opens and Fiona's mother, white as skim milk and looking like a slattern in a side-draped Hawaiian print, says, "Don't want any," before she realizes Fiona is by the boy's side so they can't be salesmen.

"This is . . ." begins Fiona.

"Don't want any," her stepgrandmother yells from inside.

"Shut up," her mother says over her shoulder into the interior behind her, dark except for a blue gleam from the television.

"This is my . . ." says Fiona.

"What y'all ringing the doorbell for?" Fiona's mother asks her.

"I said, shut up," the old lady says again, and Fiona can see her figure crouched and outlined in the blue light from the screen. Her face is all but pressed to it.

140

"Fiona, y'all ought to learn to assert yersef," says her mother in a Missouri twang.

"This is my friend, Jack Pine," says Fiona, following her mother inside.

"Shut up, shut up," says the stepgrandmother. "Cain't heah."

"Shut up yersef," says her mother. "This yere is Fiona's friend.

"Y'all set down," she says, letting the screen door crash closed. Its bottom flares out in a bulge of loose wire fringe and caresses Jack's trousers in a whispering sound of snagging as he edges past her mother, whose dress is rucked up in the back, revealing clumps of blue veins spraying up the backs of her chalk-white legs.

Jack takes the chair near the front door, an on-his-mark attitude of readiness for quick escape in case the visit goes against him, as he obviously feels it may very well do, what with the sounds of a second harangue going on over the main event at the television.

Altercating contenders are the rule for Fiona, but now she sees much too late what a shock it all must be for a stranger. The prime noise comes from the old woman before the play on the set. She casts censoring looks at them and mutters a steady series of "shut up, shut up, shut up," aimed at Jack, Fiona, and her mother. In the corner, over coffee and cigarettes, sits an older neighbor woman with Fiona's stepcousin, and his mother, Fiona's stepaunt. They argue. There is another argument on the soap opera the old woman is listening to.

The old woman's "shut ups" begin to have a sordid, soothing charm, like the steady tick of a clock. The neighbor woman is telling the aunt, "Y'all heard Fairiss say he wants a job, ain't his fault," as she takes the part of the boy whose aspect and sunken posture is one of oppression, defeat, and hopefully quick death. Jack looks at him and away again. Fiona can see by the horseshoe shape of her aunt's jaw that she is choosing between swatting and continuing to feed this son of hers.

"Over there's Fiona's aunt, Miz Koohunga," says her mother to Jack by way of introduction, "and that's her cousin, Fairiss. Miz Farr's a neighbor visitin'."

"Shut up," says the stepgrandmother.

"That's Mr. Epts's mother, and a sight of care she is too; taken to wettin' at night."

"He says he wants a job," the aunt hisses, making up her mind about further nurturing. "A damn lie and a laugh."

"I aim to have me a car," says the cousin in his dead, beaten voice.

"Y'all shouldn't speak to him that way," says the neighbor.

"Go home," says the aunt. "He's no damn business of yersef."

"Shut up," says the old woman.

She extends a skinny arm and turns up the sound. The actress in the play howls, "Mother, he's asked for a divorce."

"And you have consented, my dear?"

"Mother, what shall I do? My marriage is finished."

"You must work it out. Anything else is a sad confession of failure," thunders the actress playing the mother.

"Necessary sacrifice," roars another actress playing family friend. "Have a nice talk with the minister," she screams.

Organ music quavers up and blasts out over the shouting announcer.

142

"Turn that damned thing off," Fiona's mother shouts. "I want to visit with Fiona's friend."

"Let's go," says Fiona.

Outside they hear another voice, hoarse with nagging. "Y'all kin hand me the nail, bonehead, son of a she-shoat. Taken after yer old woman, dumbest broad ever come off the pike. Now, thet hammer, right there. A knuckle sandwich in the teeth ain't gonna mek me no never mind."

Her stepfather in this real nightmare strains to hold aloft a shiny television antenna while her aunt's second son, about twelve, crawls about the royal blue shingled roof, patched here and there with green tar shingles.

"Now y'all dropped the wire! Kee-rist, wishen I had me some hep I kin use."

"Hey there," he calls to Fiona, who is trying to duck out of sight.

"This is Jack," she says, and walks him away from the whole mess. So she's young, dumb, and stupid, but Jack speaks nicely and someday she wants to talk the way he does, not like her family. She can't do anything about color, but she can do something about other things. What—right here, today, sitting drinking too much coffee, smoking too many cigarettes—has this industry on her part got for her? So she talks and acts like a gentlewoman, and she's still black, still a loser, and now on the run.

Later, when Jack comes home from his private school, his folks, still afraid of her, buy him a new car and a driver's education course at eight dollars an hour, but she meets a few boys not so easy to contain and her stepfather and his friends in Klan and Legion get a message across to her mother that her daughter, Fiona, will be happier elsewhere.

143

Fiona is a threat, so she is threatened in turn. She is not ordered away; she is encouraged not to hang about and wreck the chances of the rest. Her beat is to become a city one, teeming with noise, smell of smog, feel of grit in teeth and eyes, and taste of metallic muck in her mouth. Stir like hell and add a steady psychic fear, and there is Fiona's life and hard times.

She opens the back door and is rewarded by a fresh, salt-scented breeze. Now that she is faced by stormy crisis in her life, nature provides a climate contrary to her personal black outlook. Today dawns fair and promises beauty of sunshine and peace in contrast to the hurricane that brews inside her mind.

Tonight, if she can find sanctuary, the climate will be all disaster—fire, bullets, and shock. The perverseness of witch-like nature.

She pours another cup of coffee and lights another cigarette. George. It comes back to him, everything. What does she know about his work?

She knows where the building is, but most of it is underground, so what has she seen?

She knows there are guards stationed at the only door, that he wears a badge with his picture on it like millions of other men in many other types of work. So what?

She also knows that on his way out of the city, when he stops by for a quick one, as he calls it, he places a beige pigskin brief case down beside the bed. Within it are papers, but she does not look at them. He handles top-secret documents to do with defense. She also knows he stages things at places called sectors about the country. He goes to Japan, Hawaii, Norway, Denmark, and even Turkey, because she has seen ticket stubs and sometimes tickets.

144

She knows he sees other women in other cities, and that he often plays poker with the boys. She knows he is a valuable man, since he dreams up things given to military people.

She knows there is an expensive computer in his building and that his corporation hires physicists, psychologists, and mathematicians. George is a math type. She understands a representative of a government like China might be interested in information from a man like George. She also understands why an agent of this government would hope to catch a man like George if he is selling or giving away secrets.

But . . . what she can't figure out is how she can even be considered in this private action among other people. Of what use is she, Fiona, to any of them? She must examine it all over once again. Let's say Humel wishes to use her association with George as a threat to expose George, blackmail him into telling secrets. But his wife already knows. Even George's boss likes women the way George does, so he can't care less about George's girl friends; he's too busy with his own. If George has said good-by to her, there's no way she can get him back again even to please the agent, and/or Humel.

She has no claim on George. But wait. Maybe Humel has in mind one of these torture sessions so graphically described in books and portrayed in movies. Say he hopes to get George right here and work Fiona over like the Gestapo to make George talk. God, that's frightening even to think of! But George will simply turn him in to the cops, and he won't kill George because then there won't be any chance to make him talk. . . . Oh, God, she simply can't bear to think about it at all; it's far too nerve-wracking. God, she hopes never to see the miserable, trouble-making George again. She isn't safe around him. He knows too much for her own good. But Humel will turn her in if she doesn't get George back somehow; a short call to cops.

She might be able to make a pretense of getting George back, yes; but she's already been turned in and counted up by the agent. What about that? Well, then, Humel can still dope her up and make good a threat to ship her off to his country for the white slavers and make a packet of money on her too. Hell, this is no joke, the traffic in white slavery is big money and it's everywhere. Yes, she must run and hide in Watts in hopes they can't get in to follow there.

Now there's John, the agent. Why does he bother with her? Why does he not simply go after George or Humel and nail them and leave her alone? Who knows? She doesn't, that's for sure. It's a mystery.

For another thing, she swears George hasn't even laid eyes on this damned Humel. But John, the agent, says she must get George back so the agent can use her as a witness to help him nail Humel and probably also crucify George, who is innocent except for being keen on war, which pleasure or sin he shares with many.

Why does the agent need Fiona to keep on with George? Does he suspect George too? Does he need George's help to catch Humel and capture his intricate spy ring? It has to be the star-witness thing slated for Fiona on all counts. Then she'll be crucified and finished, once exposed in the white glare of a court of law. Finished! They'll hang the entire case on the shreds of her ruined life. She'll be a captive rather than an exile. . . .

The telephone screams into the early-morning deadly silence of the house. Fiona jumps so much her cigarette spills crazily from her rigid fingers and rolls along the floor. She follows it, smashes it out by the stove, and moves, as though being shadowed, through the sitting room to the phone.

"Hello," she says hoarsely.

There's only the sound of heavy breathing.

"Sure, here I am," she screams with nerves crackling like tinder. "Yes, I'm here," she adds, and cracks the phone back to its cradle.

Shaking, heart thumping, she runs back to the kitchen. Surely the garbage truck will come soon. If the phone rings again, she must answer; they must not suspect she's gone; not yet. They are just checking, that's it. If it rings again, she will say calmly, "I am here."

Ah, at last, the rumble of gears grinds down the court. The garbage truck is coming. She slips outside and through the back gate and stands waiting by the fence. All is early-morning quiet. Even Grampaw has stopped complaining about dogs to pass his time. The truck, in low gear, creeps closer. It stops beside Fiona and a lithe young black boy jumps lightly to the ground from the running board. She goes around the front of the truck to the older black man at the wheel; she has a fifty-dollar bill in her hand.

"Will you send a taxi with a black driver here for me after dark tonight? I must go to Watts," she says.

"Sure, sister, glad to. Y'all don't have to pay nothing; glad to, my cousin drives a cab."

"Please, do take it for your family, okay?"

"Thanks, but I don't like takin' your money; it don't cost you nothin'; y'all one of us, sister."

"I would like you to have it and thank you so much.

About eight, please. Ask him to drive down but not stop here, and not to honk, please; just slow down at the bottom of the Court and then I'll get down to him, please."

"Sure, okay, and thanks," he says.

Fiona darts back inside and the steady clatter of cans and lids crashing back, slamming on, and banging down gradually fades away to silence once more.

Now, right now, while there is time, she ought to plan something foolproof by way of quick finish for her nemesis, George. Because, just as in the days of her youth, she is a threat. To George's job? To his wife? The agent? Who? Why? The point is that she, in turn, is threatened. Someone is out to get Fiona. Who? Why?

By the way, who told the agent where she would be handy to meet at the Mar Vista on Friday night—last night? Who knew Fiona would be there? George knew! George telephoned her there. To make sure of her presence? Where George, the officer, is concerned, the troops, the human matériel, are the most readily expendable of all in war.

16
Saturday, August 14. 10:00 A.M.

She stands on the soft, fluffy orange rug of the bedroom. Then she smooths the bedspread, patting over it to remove even the hint of rest from its pristine surface. She polishes away the light film of dust on the maple dressing table and moves the silver ring case and button hook to the exact center of its shiny surface. She fluffs the yellow shades on the lamps that are like a ballerina's tutu of gathered silk, twitches out the copper corduroy curtains to their fullest drape, and draws together the sheer undercurtains of pale orange silk, closing out the early-morning view of all the poison plantings in the wild garden.

No, not for George. This will be as though she leaves a sign reading: "Murdered by Fiona James, of 92 Seconna Place, Venice." No, with great cunning, craft, and guile she must devise a trap to do away with George.

Let's say she calls Humel before slipping away this evening and she tells him, "I have news for you. George came last night and will sell you information. He says you must meet him in Watts at this address." She can get an address from the black cab driver. She can tell Humel she

149

will call him back to tell him what it is. It might be a café, anyplace, just so it's inside Watts.

"I can't go to Watts," Humel may reply.

"That's your affair, how you can get in there," she'll say. "Perhaps you can find a blackface in there to help you," she might advise.

"Why does George decide to help me?" he may ask.

"He needs money badly; he wants a divorce," she can tell him. "It will take quite a lot of money to get his wife to agree."

"And what do you want?" he may ask.

"To be left alone."

Yes, it might work—and then to John, the agent: "Yes, George wants out; he wants to meet you at this address," she can say.

"Out of what?" the wily agent may ask.

"He's afraid."

"Of whom?"

"Of Humel, his crowd, the whole situation; says they've threatened his family. They may gun him down if they think he plans to tell you about them."

It might work. She can almost smell freedom. Somehow she must get George to the address and make it look as though his accidental death is that of an unfortunate victim, all the shooting going on, maybe believed to be a looter? Don't be silly! A National Guard Colonel in full uniform looting! No, she can be the looter; he can appear to be apprehending her. Guns will fire from Guardsmen, police, and snipers too. Maybe even Humel and his pals will use their guns. God, she can all but swear George will be at least wounded in the fray. She can manage a stray bullet for him herself, if it comes to that.

Does the agent really think George confides secrets to her? What a laugh! Say he reels off coded computer tapes at her. Say he's got stock in American oil or tin or something in Vietnam and pays money to the Viet Cong for protection of same. Say George is up to here in graft and corruption. So what? If so, what of it? She knows not one thing about it. No, the agent wants her as a prize witness; that has to be it.

She knows George works at something requiring a man to be investigated and cleared. She knows he has access to safes that hold documents because he sometimes says, "Be a little late. Stand by. My night to check locks on all the secrets in the safes."

She does know this much. Now, how can this give aid and comfort to so-called enemies? It is the witness thing, something she can better get along without.

Leave no sign of escape plans around. And pack only the little overnight case of wicker with a change of underclothing. Hide it under the bed even now, with no one here. No, not the bed. Better behind the tapestry screen in the corner of the sitting room. There. So what if she takes only a change of underclothing from her splendid wardrobe? If all goes well, she'll be right back here and settled down again with a new man; and she will do the interrogating this time, first off, better believe it.

Second thoughts: Better put in a clean blouse and the thin wool dressing gown of black flannel with the satin binding, and shower slippers too, although she's heard how few bathrooms there are in Watts. Still, just in case. . . .

Now a survey of the whole house; it must be left behind her with no shocked look of scrambling haste to escape. All neat and clean. She is only out for the evening.

She even examines the tiny hall where, in the white-painted niche traced with gold trim, stands the white Princess telephone, its long extension cord coiled beneath it, that lights up when the receiver is lifted. Is it time to make calls? No, too early in the morning; ten thirty; ought to wait at least until noon; it will look too eager.

The sitting room—where the cushions are neat, the books and magazines put away in the wicker basket with the gold velvet pillow top—looks smart. A shame to leave it even temporarily. The curtains are drawn tight. Oh, better get that thin glaze of dust from beneath the Franklin stove. The dustmop disperses it nicely. Ashtrays are clean, brass bright and shiny; copper nut bowl holds no careless shells. A quick glance at the peaceful, make-believe scene on the television. Should she turn it on and check the riot's progress. . . . Oh, no—a knock at the door. The front door? This is frightening. Who comes to the front door? No one.

Fiona jumps again when the front doorbell rings. Must be a stranger. The police with a warrant? The agent says he will fix that. George's wife with a gun? George says he'll take care of her. Humel's pals?

She moves softly over the thick hemp of the border rug to the center rug of gold, and leans on the sofa to peer through the crack left in the drawn curtains.

Two small black boys stand on her doorstep. She almost giggles in relief. She wrenches the door open; it creaks in protest. They look up at her, both smoking long wet-looking cigar butts. She takes the chain off the door and opens it wider, "Hi," she says.

"Hi," they chime, removing the cigars. "Say, lady, y'all want to buy some nice curtins?"

"Come in," she says.

152

"Nice curtins, brand-new," the taller one says, while both look eagerly about them. "Y'all rich for a colored lady," the boy says candidly. "Sure is a pretty place y'all got."

"Thank you," she says, fingering the sleazy, cheap, and stringy panel curtains of wispy material. In spite of the extra dose of sizing they've been given at birth to stiffen them, she knows one wash will remove it and she'll have a rag. Up in the corner of each of the four there is a store price tag with size, tax, and price neatly listed in red. Looted from Watts, from Stevens's department store, a cheap version of a dime store and a regular cartel of them in less desirable living areas strung all over southern California. Four white panel curtains at $4.98 each.

"All right, I'll take them," she says.

The boys grin in delight and replace the cigar butts in their mouths when she hands them a twenty-dollar bill. "Keep the change, men. Big deal!" she laughs.

"Say, lady, y'all sure nuff got a swell layout here," says the taller boy. "How come y'all live with Whitey?" he asks.

"I am about to move," she says.

"Y'all can move to Watts. It's swinging now, boy—all them wars, free booze, everything."

"Where do you live?" she asks.

"We lives with our folks at Eighty-seven and Figueroa," he says.

"Is that an apartment?"

"Yepper."

"Maybe I'll come by and see you tonight. Would you like me to come?" she asks.

"Sure nuff; y'all come. We ain't got much food and like that. When we leaves, didn't even have no bread in the house. We buy some now. We got to sneak back into

Watts oursefs too. Our old man's got plenty of free booze now; he don't care about nothing. Wow! Should see all them fires burning everything down."

"I'll bring some food with me if you like. Treats!"

Oh, she feels so free and good just talking with these kids.

"Okay. My mother ain't been home two nights running now. She can't get by them road blocks. She don't get off from Whitey's house till after curfew that come on at eight."

"I'll come by before that. Okay?"

"Okay," they say. " 'Bye."

"See you later. 'Bye." She relocks the door.

She'll take a large sack of groceries. There's all the ham and bread too, she's got on hand for the new gentleman friend who turns out to be John, the agent. Now it will feed a family.

Into the deep cuff of the raincoat she tucks the boy's address printed inside a match packet. After inserting it there, she pats the cuff and it crinkles a snapping sound back at her.

Fantastic, how much she's come to detest George in a few hours. Just as much as Humel. If she felt like helping anyone now besides herself, it would be John, the agent, because he's the only one of the three who hasn't got war on the brain.

Why do people hate one another enough to go to war? Because of skin color, that's why. If they don't match, kill 'em. That's what it's all about basically, no matter how they dress it up in politics.

If she can be made dictator, she will end war in a rush. For a start she'll send every Vietnamese family a gorgeous

154

water buffalo. To him the animal is a new car, a ranch house with double garage, and religious freedom, whatever the brand. Yes, even fortune-telling like her mother will not only be permitted, it will be the law. She'll send buffalos instead of soldiers. And she won't fence off any nation and refuse to speak, like a bad boy in solitary confinement. Rather, she will cultivate bad boys until there is peace everywhere, even with those whose skin doesn't match. She'll make them all lazy and decadent, and smother them with ice boxes and fur coats and two bathrooms and lots of food. She'll put scientists to work to invent something for pregnant women to take, guaranteed to make each newborn child the exact shade of skin as every other child on the entire planet—say a pale beige for everyone.

Hell, who will pay any attention to her? No one. She is a mean, arrogant, pushy black, like the ones Whitey talks about. Whitey, on the other hand, is kindly, patient, understanding, and mostly liberal—liberals to a man—the kind Hitler hated.

Kill the liberals like Fiona, he said. Yes, she's a liberal. What else can she be? Pity she can't start being liberal with herself. Vengeance is mine, says this mulatto, Fiona. Kill Whitey. Start with George.

Think how I refrain from leading only sons of nice Whitey families up the garden path to marriage, how I've refrained from writing letters to wives, always refused to embarrass my employers in any way, in fact. Where has my sweet, discreet attitude got me? Close to prison, that's where. I could land there yet. It's time I adopt another policy altogether, far more on the primitive side. Kill or be killed. War.

People with light skin will never leave those with dark

skin alone, so pack up your troubles and the groceries now. Prepare to hide out with your own kind. What am I so upset about? I will be safe. I'll ride it all out. Everything will be fine. I may be female, and black too, but I am not stupid.

Where does a robin redbreast find sanctuary? In a great flock of robin-redbreasted birds, that is where.

17
Saturday, August 14. NOON

Is is too early to begin packing up groceries? Yes, someone might come by; the agent, or Humel, someone. What can be done to pass this time except think too much? If only she could simply go home for a while. For many, a simple move in time of distress or danger. But what is the good even to think of such an idea? Useless. Masks will have to come off. She seldom gets a letter from her mother. But if some one read them, they might think Fiona a loved member of a nice family. But these niceties are only in letters posted to her miles away from the writer. If a stranger saw them, he might conclude she's on ordinary good terms with her family. But no personal contact, not with her skin color.

156

Hell, she might get pregnant. In the past she's even considered having the simple operation to prevent conception and thus dispense with contraceptive aids altogether, since this is her responsibility in the business. But what if with George she might pioneer and to hell with it all! She could claim out loud in public all about it. Think of the money, and think of having a child of her own, someone on her side. Those little black boys and their curtains, so much fun talking to them! She can enjoy such innocent admiration in the eyes of a child. A child of Fiona's, especially if it takes after her father, will photograph plenty dark. She can see the newspapers now: A poor girl's life ruined by this man George, who said he'd marry her. Can she summon up the nerve to put a child through what she's been through? Not bloody likely. It is her only saving grace, that and freedom from disease, according to visits to the tiny Jewish doctor, a discreet and kindly grandfather of a man, so polite, so nice to her without the judging nasty attitude of the average Whitey.

Isn't it too bad she isn't inclined to the Lesbian? There could be a fine female friend. In her profession there is no good looking for a girl friend. The only kind she can get are fat-breasted Lesbians covered in mannish shirts and sweaters, square skirts or pants over wide solid hips. They have muscles like grapefruit in the calves of too-short legs, ankles like boxcars, and feet in sturdy flat shoes. Females who talk too loud from mouth corners, while other girls in brittle dresses screech and kiss them in half-mad lunges, as she has seen them doing one night at a café on the ocean front. That's a place she leaves rapidly when she learns the cops make frequent calls there to put down knifing disagreements between these cohabitating females.

157

At least these women wear no masks. Everyone else does, even though Fiona is considered to be the one masked. There's a lie, because the agent is a liar; so is Humel; so is George; and so is Fiona's mother.

Her mother is the first liar, and is even now, in her lying, silly letters. There was her mother's religion. She tells Fiona Christ was murdered for it. A killer's religion, all right, because later it cost the lives of billions in two centuries of holy war fighting about it. Fiona's early years are filled with this fundamentalist frightening religion, with its terrifying mysterious God of the Old Testament and its younger God Jesus of the New. She's introduced to Hell, where she's bound to end up if she doesn't obey everything the old God says, and the young one too. In her helpless, early insecure years, this is much of her life.

Her mother tells her that Adam and Eve fell from grace and that gave them a conscience, a kind of left-handed handicap, so that from then onward all must propagate the race in guilt. With this dubious gift of a moral sense, man, in order to pick right from wrong, became infamous for being the greatest corrupting force among all animals. This is what conscience does for man: makes him the most evil of all, as anyone can read by checking the past record.

By the time Fiona is twelve, her mother is gradually giving up the idea that eating too much and weighing some two hundred pounds is any kind of godliness. She drops religion and begins to study astrology, although not accepting sex as any less a sin than she did when she substituted gluttony for it.

Her mother catalogues all of them, putting them in place for life. Fiona's stepfather is Taurus, the bull; her mother is Pisces, the fish; and her real father, the really

158

bad one, is Scorpio. Let's see. One half sister is Cancer; the other one, Sagittarius; and Fiona is Gemini. In spite of labels, they all grow up and her bull stepfather entertains the idea of leaving Missouri for Out West.

"Y'all send off some money and get the local paper," says her bull stepfather. "See what the town is like ahead a' time."

Her fish mother is against it. She can see more money in a large city for her newly found creed, astrology. "What's the population there?" she asks. "I hear less than five hundred in that dump." So how many suckers can she count on among this mangy few?

"Then the property will be cheap and low taxes. Y'all take lots of people and y'all got lots of taxes," he says.

"And no jobs, and these kids too; her too," her mother says.

Her stepfather isn't interested.

"Y'all take them charts; it won't be easy with a Cancer, a winged horse, and her, a Gemini, to take care of," says her mother.

"They can take off soon as they get out of school, and we can start to live some before we're wore out and dead— half dead today anyway, with that molasses cake weighed like stone that Cancer one built last night."

"She's a moon child."

"Y'all got a bunch of astronauts and too bad y'all can't land 'em on the moon with a swift kick. Sick of the whole shebang, three of 'em female, and her too; one too tall and skinny, one too fat and short, and one black and loose. Y'all got trouble, I say."

At fourteen, Fiona tries to find out about her father. "Who was he?" she asks.

"He was not much, sad to say."

"Then why did you hand him the most intimate attention you have to give?" she wants to ask. Instead she says, "How did he earn his living?"

"God knows! He was a mess."

Her mind reels with dammed-up questions, shouting to be asked aloud. She dares not ask them. Her mother will tell her nothing. Fiona continues the farce. What she says and does are exactly opposite of desire. Free choice is dead for Fiona. At the very least she wants to ask how dark? How old? Where did he come from? How did you meet him? What is his name?

"I'd never met anyone like that," her mother announces out of the blue one day, and mostly to herself. Fiona bends over a book pretending to read. "There is this depression on," her mother continues. "Very little to do. Annie, my friend, and I got in the way of going to town to a candy shop. . . . Oh, that was years ago. . . . Get the potatoes on, Fiona; they'll all be roaring in here in a minute and your paw too."

"Was this in Missouri?" Fiona asks.

"Y'all know it was; y'all born there."

"I thought you said I was only a baby when I left there for Indiana or someplace."

"Yes, that's it. So aggravating, all your questions. Put your mind on something else. Y'all ought to get that application in to the gas company. They are expanding and your chart says you're beginning a new twelve-year period now. Might as well be at the gas company. Y'all could work up to be a supervisor or something, your own boss. No good depending on men and marriage; what I've seen, nothing for y'all to count on."

160

Fiona makes no applications. She must start her twelve-year cycle far from home. She is extremely careful because at any time a rap sheet on her can include false passport, no birth certificate, no records, not even a Social Security number, no driver's license, library card in different name, phone number in another, unlisted. And it can include soliciting at the Mar Vista; don't forget that.

First off she gets rid of Epts. Fiona Inept, that's how she feels about that name. She goes home only once since leaving there. Her mother is skinny now; she is brittle, too —teeth, hair, even speech; lost the drawl someplace. She wears an expensive black dress and quite a lot of jangling bracelets. Her face is a road map, detailing everything from highways to little-used back trails. Her too-white face looks lumpy as clotted sour milk. The clients pay well for her line of bull.

"Forty-seven now," she tells Fiona with pride. "I've made up my mind to stay young, wear high heels, and watch the fat."

No more the sloppy mother who, when the lines were full, once spread laundry about on bushes like a gypsy camp to dry. Now she's rich and harried-looking, a professional teller of fortunes, and Fiona is asked to stay at a nearby motel.

The neighbors will think she's only a client, her mother hopes. She tells Fiona her clients must have privacy. Her mother also expects Fiona to stay mostly at the motel, or at least out of the house. "I have a full schedule now, customers the whole day long," she says. "Sometimes even half the night," she adds.

First morning of her happy homecoming Fiona is up early and walks to a café for coffee. She buys a Thermos bottle and has it filled and goes back to the motel, reads, drinks coffee, smokes cigarettes, and sends cards about a wonderful time to a current boy friend.

She walks along the old main street and talks to a waitress, who is wary of this strange skin color out before God and everybody in this small-town coffee bar in a café right smack on the main street.

Fiona fingers merchandise in a department store and many looks are cast her way because there is no other black face in the town now; even the old shoeshine man has vanished. In the local paper there is little mention of civil rights, although a three-line story does detail the fact that another "Negro" has been shot and killed down South someplace.

Fiona eats at the drugstore, takes a cab to the motel for her luggage, and then to her mother's house to say good-by.

The rain is coming down hard and she stands on the doorstep and her mother has rain dripping off the end of her snub nose. The drops trickle along the sunken bridge of it over the tip, and onto the fat tongue she holds coyly out to lick at it. Fiona has an absurd but raging desire to spear her mother's tongue with her nail file and rip down its broad length and make a string tie of it.

The taximan tells her there is nothing to do in this dump. "It's either church or the bar; take your choice," he says.

There's fortune-telling, you forget that, she ought to say.

At the train depot, she thinks of her mother's present grandeur in comparison to the way it was back then. What another world it is from Fiona at seventeen, saying that first good-by to home. She sits by the oilcloth-covered kitchen table circled by empty, mismatched chairs. There are flies everywhere; it is August and there is no air conditioning.

162

Fiona looks a wild bird of exotic plumage caught briefly in a seedy trap. She wears a rust-colored dress with black figures that look like live insects all over it. She has on black stockings and shoddy shoes. A ruffled black slip peers out beneath the skirt of this new dress that her mother points out she has spent too many dollars to buy for Fiona's going away. She wears a flat straw hat with copper ribbons. Fiona's is a floozy, blowsy outfit, and her mother keeps reminding Fiona of the sacrifice she made in order to buy it. Fiona has a thin rim of lipstick about her mouth, and she continues to bite her lips as her mother hands her an ice cube wrapped in a paper napkin so Fiona can apply it to her painfully aching head. She wishes so much that she need not go, for this—bad as it is—this is known. The unknown is fearful. But then her mother is picking up her suitcase and opening the door to fear. Away she goes! Ready or not, Fiona is on her way.

18
Saturday, August 14. 1:00 P.M.

During one of their first sessions Humel asks her, "Why are you so afraid?"

"What makes you think I am?"

It's nothing to what she's going to be today, Saturday, August 14. She is spitless with fear, mouth dry and creaking. It's a jolly good thing he isn't asking her this today. Yes, far better it was still back in those relatively peace-on-earth days, even for a Fiona. Now she can only croak and crack and whisper.

"You do agree you are afraid?" Humel persists all those light years away back then.

"Yes," she tells him. "It's mostly to help defend myself. I'm not afraid all the time, but let's say I am bright enough to feel threatened because I know I'm a threat to moral law and order. I have an intelligent fear and respect of cops and those they represent, the law-and-order rich group. They don't represent me; they're not my servants; on the contrary, they are in charge; I am their servant, a slave and pawn, in fact."

"Do you really believe that?"

"Yes, and I don't understand why more people aren't afraid too. They must be terribly ignorant. Goethe said, among many other things, 'Nothing the rabble fear more than intelligence, if they understood what is truly terrifying, they would fear ignorance.' Still, I wasn't completely frightened of cops and the law until I read a book about a good shoemaker and a poor fish peddler. Their skin wasn't even black. Upton Sinclair's 'Boston,' that was it. Afterward I thought it wasn't so much wishing I had the courage, as it was the sad fact I saw little worth having courage to face. Yes, I think that's it. It's a truly fearful world for almost anyone, and tragic because it could all be so much better. The terribly clever and the ruthlessly ambitious, who make lots of money in a country where the dollar is the meaning of life, can afford to be fearless, but

164

not the rest. One can't be too careful of mixing with ignorant police, some of whom don't know themselves what they may do next. So where does this leave me and everyone else? I should think a sociologist would be more interested in why so many young kids are disturbed, young people kill themselves, middle-aged are in mental hospitals, and many old people insane."

Sure, all that, and what good her crafty cunning at avoiding police when she can be taken in so handily by a sociologist and a government agent with no trouble for them at all?

"Do you watch television?" Humel asks her in an early interview for which she takes the tidy sum of twenty-five dollars, just as though he's the patient and she the doctor.

"Only the news," she says. "There are soap operas on all channels from eleven in the morning and I'm doing housework and special little projects. These shows go on sometimes until four and five in the afternoon, but I'm not interested in such pap."

"Would you say you went into the profession from economic cause?"

"I don't know. More likely character defect. Maybe too much religion at an early age that made me angry and made me want to punish society—or so a former client, a psychologist, told me. I would say to make a living, and if a little adventure and travel come with it, I don't mind."

"But you are not really poor then and were not brought up in an unhealthy ghetto. And you seem to have fair education or read much and appear to have a high level of natural intelligence. Still, it is a surprise to me that in this country more women of deprived early condition do not become at least low-status prostitutes," he says.

There's something about "this country" that gives her a

first inkling of a mask he may wear. Why does he say this in the condemning way? She lets it pass.

"Look, Dr. Humel . . ." she begins.

"I do not have the doctorate yet," he says. "Last month I hear about a candidate who is successful with a thesis, 'Extrinsic and Intrinsic Factors Associated with Longevity and Aging in Adult Mosquitoes.' " His laugh to accompany his wit is of the spraying variety.

"Look," she says again, "I supply a demand, perform a service. I never had social place to lose. Perhaps being in the business is a personality defect, but I don't care. I'm not a sensual woman, not eager for the sex part, but I can pretend. I didn't have a too-early sex experience; I wasn't ignorant about such things; I didn't seek the life; I moved into it, or fell into it, if you like. I don't want to humiliate men to get even with my father who deserted me, leaving me black among whites—or at least not consciously. It's a secret to me if it's revenge I'm looking for. I don't hate my mother; I pity her; she's dull and a bore. I drifted into this business, thinking—if I thought at all—that under my circumstances at the time it was all I could do. I admit I wanted attention. Had I not wanted love so much, I think I could have been a student, a good one."

"Do you know other girls on your level in this work?"

"No. I've met some; I can spot them too. And the richer the country becomes, the more high-class prostitutes there will be. Men don't marry early to get sex as they once did. In the tradition of women like me, courtesan or paramour —and I don't mean this in a bragging way—we are not meager women. One must have more to offer clever, wealthy men than sex; one must have something to say; sex is only a matter of minutes. There are many of us and our lives are

166

similar. Sex is sex—or lust, if you like—and there's not much new about it. If you've heard my story, you've heard most of us, but it's our dreams that might be different. For example, most of us want diamonds, cars, and furs; while I'd like a farm, dirty hands, too. But when you've heard the sex part, you've heard us all. It's a strange society that is so hypocritical that it creates a need and then wants to persecute us for filling it. There is in the divorce rate some indication of how many desperate marriages there are. The usual answer of wives—more children to hold a man—doesn't work. The causes of prostitution are money and more money. Men get it and have it to spend and want girls to spend it on—but not on harlots, slatterns in thick make-up and tawdry dress.

"Jesus singled out the whore for special mention and consideration, so one can have religion too, if desired. Other women are no different than me; they trade for a ring—and then breed. I won't do that if I'm careful, and they shouldn't, with the population the way it is. So, married or not, we're the other gender—sex. All the talk about freedom for woman and developing her mind is a lie; she is sex. The male has the mind prerogative.

"I live here quite happily in this four-block white ghetto, except I hear voices saying jigs are moving in and taking over. 'Sambo is crowding us,' they say. 'But with luck,' they add, 'we'll be dead by the time they take over.' I only made it in here because a friend found the place and paid the rent. The landlord saw me later and liked the way I'd slaved to fix it up, so when I leave, he can ask a higher rent. The lower orders among us animated dolls are caught in a revolving door between jail and street, but a person on the higher scale, like myself, is well read, intelligent, perceptive, and sympathetic. Sometimes I think my color started me—too many brick walls to climb."

"Do you use drugs?"

"Never. I protect and preserve myself for the job. Rich men can have the best of the most, so I keep up. It helps as well to be a good liar, not only to customers but to myself. The truth won't make me free, though actually life becomes bearable when I lie. But if I'm a liar, what are the clients? We are together in this. I don't seek debasement. My demeanor is studied. I supply the stimulation of change and I make a living. I'm a good Dutch housewife, thrifty and inventive. I watch my money and spend it carefully, except for good food and drink, which are part of doing a good job. We all wear a mask, of course—even upright wives and mothers, most of whom have just as many emotional problems as I have. I guess I am what I am more through chance than through anything else."

Yes, you feed all this, and more, week in and week out, into his little bug in the pipe bowl; for a few miserable dollars you risk the chance of going to prison for years, on income-tax evasion alone. And take pride in it too; that is why you are caught, get to feeling pretty cocky reeling off all this sermon to an attentive male listener. Now you'd better get on with it and try to get yourself out of the trap your own conceit put you in. My God, it's two o'clock. Put in the call to the agent first, then call Humel.

She dials and a man answers. "Yes?"

"I wish to leave my name, Fiona."

"Okay," says the voice, and the receiver clicks in her ear.

She hangs up. When will the agent return the call? Who knows? Try to rest a bit. She lies on the sofa, feet up, and closes her eyes. She listens to humming noises in her head.

She rests in that state of suspended animation marked by feeling too strung up and nervous for an actual doze and too tired out to be fully awake. In this gloaming she feels the tingling, prickling sensation experienced when she puts on the black raincoat. There is a flicking touch on the bottoms of her feet. Someone is standing there. She can feel the shadow of someone even through closed eyes. Tap, tap against the bare soles of her feet goes a finger. She peeks through the screen of her thick lashes. God, she opens her eyes wide at John, the agent. She wants to scream at him, "Have you never heard of knocking?"

People in her weak position are far more circumspect than that. She says, "Oh," and sits up.

"I'd like a few words with you," he says, utterly poised. He is accustomed to sneaking into people's houses, so his manner proclaims. "You didn't hear my knock," he lies coolly.

"Because you didn't," Fiona wants to say, "and besides, the door is locked; it is always locked."

"The door wasn't locked," he lies.

She says nothing. Her cards are all lousy; no cards to play at all.

Ah, she can say she's just called him and pretend with him he doesn't know it. The watching of her house now must be super secure.

"I have just called you," she says.

"Why?" he asks, pretending not to know, the liar.

"George was here last night."

"He came back?"

"Yes."

"He wasn't in Watts with the Guard?"

"He slipped out, I guess; he didn't say."

169

"That couldn't have been easy." He didn't believe her. "What did you call me for?"

"George wants to see you. He'll be at this address in Watts at ten tonight." She scribbles it on a page of a scratch pad and hands it to him.

"About what?"

"He didn't say. I think he could be mixed up in something and wants out. Or maybe he wants to tell you about Humel."

"And why in Watts?"

"I guess because of his duty there. Maybe he thinks Humel or one of his friends will be after him there."

"What for? They are more interested in George alive," he answers, cool as lettuce.

Please let him half-believe her at least.

"I don't know. Maybe you can call him, but he said that is where he will be and that he wants to talk to you about something. That's all I know."

"Where are you planning to go?"

"Nowhere."

"That's right. You stay here until we get this all sorted out."

"They say there are Communists running the riot in Watts. Maybe George knows Humel is part of that, I don't know."

Shut up and say nothing more.

"There's a tap on your phone now."

God, she'll have to go out in daylight and make a call to Humel at the pay booth, or, worse yet, the open-air thing with side flaps on the boulevard by the grocery store, and the agent will have someone to see this too. Or maybe—

just maybe—she can get the taximan to stop. Well, her life is one big complicated mess now.

"I wonder why you are interested in me?" she asks him.

"We want you as a witness, against both George and Humel."

"There's a warrant out for me. George's wife signed it."

"That can be taken care of."

There's the law's an ass for you, as Dickens said. What else can it be, since it is man-made?

"I see."

"Excuse me, I'll take a look through if you don't mind."

Mind? That will do me much good.

"What are you looking for?"

"Tickets to someplace, that kind of thing."

He doesn't look behind the screen; please, don't let him. He turns her handbag out. Nothing. He checks the dresser drawers, the notations on the pad by the phone, and moves to the bookcases, where he riffles the pages of books.

"Paine, Dumas," he says. "You have quite a taste, or were they here when you moved in?"

"No, they're mine, mostly secondhand," she says abjectly.

"Good-by then. . . . Oh, by the way, had any visitors or calls?"

"No."

"How about a couple of Negro kids this morning?"

"Oh!" She laughs. "Yes, I forgot that. Gave them candy."

"What did they want?"

"Selling something, I've forgotten—magazines or something."

"Stolen goods, something like curtains?" he raps out.

"Yes."

"Did you buy?"

"Yes, I usually do when children come." Have the boys been forced to tell him about her big mouth mentioning her moving?

"I see." He stands by the bedroom closet. He opens the padded doors. He pulls at the skirt of the raincoat hanging up in the closet. It eludes his grasp and swishes back into the closet with a rustling sigh. He snatches at it again, shakes it. The match cover stays inside the deep cuff. Why didn't she tear that up? She knows the address and now so does he. So he finds it tucked away in there, like that, he'll know she is up to something. Fool. But it stays there.

He closes the closet doors. "I will appreciate an intelligent witness. . . . Have you heard from Humel?"

"No."

"You probably won't," he says.

He leaves by the back door as quietly as he came in. Fiona does not intend to tell him about the early-morning telephone call from the heavy breather, even though it must have come from Humel.

PART SIX

19
Saturday, August 14. 4:00 P.M.

By now her mind is in actual pain trying to figure out what she can do. Mark well the agent's slight impediment of speech, the sensitive mouth, dangerous beneath the almost twisted nose. Cruel? Yes. There's no shred of compassion in this face. He is an automatist and reminds her of George.

Remember the long-ago peaceful day on which you met George? She sits on a soft davenport in the lobby of the Mar Vista. She waits to be called to a table in the dining room. George, the stranger, leans over and extends a magazine. "Care to look at this while you're waiting?"

All the beginnings with strangers, she knows them all. "Thank you," she says, taking it. He stares at the gold ring on her finger. "Nice ring," he says. "Where did you get it?"

176

"A gift," she tells him, "from an artist friend."

He stares at her. "What's your name?"

"Fiona James."

"I'm George Aiken."

There's the innocent way she begins with George. And now she ends up reduced to this frantic state. She's alone, and at war against all the rest of the world ranged on the other side. No one is on her side. Peace is war, they say; war is peace; and it's true too. She may be the death of love, but war is the death of man. All her dodging, feinting, and ducking won't help her win this war. Humel is out to get her too. Why did he, of them all, have to turn out to be a spy? And intrigue is not her forte; she is too excitable for that. And she's a victim of shock tactics: Strike first at the unaware. She is struck, all right. The reason there is war is because people want war; they love to strike. It is glorious to fight for a country and for yourself and to leave bits of yourself on blood-drenched ground. People want war, so they get it. Only she wants peace, but there are not enough like her. Peace is not permitted. Cops are warriors; people want them to do what they do. They even wish to join in with them at the game of war. Cops make courtrooms out of streets and hold trials there and administer punishment. They always strike first, smack a person with a vagrancy charge if he has the look of owning no property that is taxable. But if she can just buy something and pay taxes, then maybe she will be safe. Yes, in war, the stronger you are, the more you have, the more it is your right to strike first. Simple defense and security; hit first and ask questions later.

She dials Humel's number. To hell with phone taps. Let

listeners hear about arrangements for George and Humel. All the better. "Yes," Humel says with his accent on the s becoming a hiss.

"This is Fiona. George was here last night."

"Yes," he says again.

"He wants to see you."

"And?"

"He needs money."

"Where does he wish to meet?"

She repeats the Watts address.

"Arrangements will be made," he says, and hangs up.

So they will be there. Now to get George there and herself too. But she has a taxi coming. That will take care of part of the problem.

When in doubt, a cat washes. She will have a soothing bath and think and scheme. She will put the chain lock on the back door. She gathers bath oil and salts, also her favorite Sandalwood soap from India, and plenty of towels. She pins up her hair, strips off her clothes, and runs water almost to the top of the tub. Then she is in it and sitting in the warm, bubbly water, sniffing the scent of flowers. Wonderful. She lies back, gazing at the chalk-white ceiling. She has worked hard to decorate this house. It is sad to leave it, even temporarily. When she first arrives here, it's a mess of swamp-green paint all over—three shades of swamp throughout the house—and broken tiles and bits of crummy carpet here and there on all the floors.

Now the bathroom is all brown, white, and silver, and opulent fat crystal jars of perfume and oil glitter along silver and glass shelves. The rug is wall to wall, dark brown and thick. A Mexican silver, star-shaped mirror twinkles on the white wall. Silver ribbon and leaves decorate white lace shower curtains, and silver bars graced with fleur-de-lis are hung with thick brown towels along the wall. The padded door shutting her in here is covered in brown velvet and studded with silver nailheads; there are frosty white fluted crystal lamps on either side of the mirror, and the shower hooks are formed of silver flowers. She eyes it all in delight; she knows the business of beauty in decor, and for pennies she makes the entire house elegant.

First two coats of white paint all over. She calls the employment agency for help. The first man looks mean and wears a string tie and a vest decorated with food droppings. The next has eyes of flint and wants too much money. And the third, a smart-ass type who hates blacks, turns the job down when he sees whom he'll be working for. She does it all herself.

Why does she call Humel on a bugged phone? The agent says he'll record all her calls. Well, he might as well hear her call to Humel because she wants the agent there tonight too. He may want to come even more if he hears Humel is coming. Yes, it may all work out. Perhaps this time tomorrow night she will be able to sink back out of sight and into her life before this mess that looks by comparison so heavenly. That long time ago before she's even heard of George. Neither the agent nor Humel will be interested in Fiona if George is dead.

Will the taxi come tonight? Yes, the garbagemen are honorable men. They are poor enough to be honest still. A thief, as anyone should be able to figure out in seconds, is a rich man. This is how he becomes rich; he is cleverer at thieving than poor men.

I am running ahead of danger just like the poor, wretched female wolf on the television. Why not take out this news incident and with some bravery look square at it? Stop wincing away from it and have done with it? She shivers in cowardly fashion in the cooling water.

Time to get out, dress, and make the bundle of groceries. She can leave them just inside the back gate. She can pretend to be emptying garbage. Of course John's men are watching her. Humel's, too, no doubt. How else did John know the boys are selling stolen curtains? And the small wolf runs and runs, she thinks again in spite of herself. Only when it is wounded does it stop to take a futile lick at itself. The blood seeps from the tiny hole and glitters. A second bullet all but spins it about, and then it scrambles to its feet again and runs until it is finished and peppered with bullets. . . . The water drains from the tub thirstily and gurgles with finality down the pipe.

A dog is howling outside. It keens and bays to itself. In its weary, foreboding cry is all the anguish of the world. Soon the old man will begin to swear, and the old woman will swear back at him. A door slams in the next house and she jumps. A truck goes up the Court, snorting and backfiring.

In the kitchen she takes out a plate of ham, and wraps it in foil. She takes pickles, a whole Holland cheese, green onions, a roll of liverwurst, salami, two loaves of rye and one of French bread, a pound of butter, and a jar of mustard from the refrigerator and puts it all on the table. She adds a half-loaf of gingerbread, two cans of cocktail sausages, and starts packing them carefully into a double grocery sack. She puts the curtains inside too, rolled up tightly. Why not give them back and let the boys sell them again if they like?

She wears the black slacks, shirt, and scarf, opens the door to look over the entire yard. There by the fence grows a tall firethorn shrub. She carries in one hand the garbage pail and in the other the sack of groceries.

When she arrives at the tall shrub, she allows the sack to slip to the ground and kicks it underneath. She opens the back gate with a noisy click of the latch and rattles the lid on the can. She clatters the small container on the side of the can and claps the lid back on with a crash. When she enters her yard again, she stops and pretends to shake something from the pail, but actually to check the exact location of the groceries. They lie there concealed.

In the house she puts her overnight case into the empty garbage pail; goes out again with it. By the gate she allows the case to drop to the ground kicking it toward the bush. Again she goes out the gate to rattle the empty pail against the can as though emptying it. Back inside the gate, she shoves the overnight case further under the bush and returns to the house.

She stands in the kitchen just back of the yellow curtains and stares at the back court, waiting for someone to appear.

According to the kitchen clock, she is rewarded for her vigilance in exactly three minutes by the sight of a man shuffling along the Court, head down, hat over his eyes as though he's been drinking. He looks just like the shambling man of last week who followed her about on that abortive shopping trip to Santa Monica. When he arrives at her gate, he openly raises the lid of her garbage can and noisily slams it down after staring into it for a few seconds. The enemy is bold as brass. Therefore it deals from massive strength. He does not open her back gate. But there's a close watch on her every movement, for sure. Darkness is her one hope. That and her own darkness. Maybe, at last, it can prove an asset rather than a liability.

With the scarf tied like a hood over her head and part of her beige face, and with black clothing, perhaps she can get into the cab and out of here in spite of all of them. Too bad there is no helicopter to come over and lift her straight up into the air. She must figure out a way to make it into that cab.

There isn't any way except in darkness. Can she lie close to the thornbush, along with the overnight case and the groceries? No, it is not possible to get that close to this bush, the thorns are too long and too sharp. But say she crouches down there near it so she can spring up fast and be inside the cab and speeding off before the enemy can get to cars and overtake her? Yes, maybe she can do this! She must. It is her only chance.

At last the brilliant ball of sun drops behind the hills in the west; only last fading streaks of pink and orange fingers trace across her alert, anxious eyes as she stares into the retreating rays, urging them to disappear faster. Then she sees only an afterglow where the sun has been. She blinks her eyes and slips on the black raincoat with its tiny rhinestones sprayed along collar and cuffs. Her eyes, still dazzled from the sunrays, make the stones look alive and winking. It is too gay for this journey, but it's dark. Curiously, she does not experience the usual reaction as she slips it on. Why does it not lift all the little downy hair along her arms? Strange, it feels so friendly, even kindly to her skin, which barely trembles in its all-encasing clasp. She ties the belt. She puts the scarf on her head, pulls the ends down about her chin, crosses them and ties them at the back of her neck.

Darkness descends swiftly, like a well-oiled curtain. A street light three doors down the Court winks on. There is none, thank God, by the back gate. The raincoat rustles companionably as she moves to the door. What a flashy coat it is! She hates the tacky look, even for this assignment. . . . Please don't clutter up an alert mind with nonsense at this critical time.

In the living room she lifts the edge of the hemp rug and removes a tiny pistol. Walt, the psychology friend before George, this is his farewell present to her. How funny, she thought at the time, saying thank you. Maybe there's more to psychology than she knows. She puts the pistol in her purse. No pins, bracelets, ruffles mar her sleek appearance. She looks a poor 'nigger' and no mistake—or maybe a neat, uppity one. But even if she meets a black and white car loaded with white-faced men in black and white uniforms, the kind that have a white stripe up the legs of the trousers, there will be no mistaking her for a white girl. No, she must not be noticed at all by anyone. The black driver must get her inside Watts before curfew. She has an address to go to and groceries to carry to prove she is only going to a black's house. But she is already strung up with fear. The police wear such shiny black boots, the leather is so polished, they remind her of very black skin. The boots are so often on top of black people where one can hardly see them at all. Black on black! When black boots kick black bodies, who knows or cares? She is frightened, but she slips out the back door to listen. Nothing is moving out there in the blackness. She creeps low along the walk and crouches by the bush. She feels about until she locates the overnight case and the sack of food.

Still stooping low, she reaches up and lifts the latch on

the gate without making a sound. Head down, she stops and then, still stooping over, creeps slowly down the Court. She listens. She watches with longing for a glimpse of a car's headlights and for the lighted arc on top proclaiming it's a taxi.

She hopes the driver has the good sense to turn off that light. Nothing is moving until a cat appears, sniffing and rubbing its way down the Court against fences, cans, and bushes. The air reeks of the stench of spilled garbage that missed the scoop of the big truck only this morning. It is years away now.

There is a fiery glow in the sky in the direction of south Los Angeles. She should have checked the riot on the news, but she didn't turn the radio on; it makes so much noise. Today it has seemed vitally important to listen continuously and to make no sound at all.

The boulevard is almost silent. The good citizens are inside their houses, content and stimulated by the uprising and the endless coverage provided by television, radio, and newspapers. The newsmen are giving every moment of time to the riot, doing their damnedest to fill up the hours with more publicity than the rioters will ever know again. Good citizens have locked the doors and sit with guns at hand, happy with a chance to defend their homes from invading armies of the dissatisfied. Citizens hope someone will come along and start something, challenge them. Really, it's wonderful the way the riot has broken up the long-hot-summer boredom of dull lives. Vietnam is too far away after all. But this is here and now, handy-like, a ringside seat. They say, "The swine must be taught a lesson. Damned filthy pigs, we'll give them an uprising. Give them niggers an inch and they want the country. Here's the thanks we get for voting

184

for civil rights. Glad I voted against that state housing bill."

There, at last, dim headlights are coming down the Court, moving along at medium speed, bumping over the broken paving, light out on top. It must be the cab. Yes, there is a dark face of a black man at the wheel. A cap is low on his forehead. The cab stops and the door swings open wide beside her.

"You it, lady?"

She leaps in, closing the door softly. "Go fast," she whispers, "and keep going, no matter what. But obey the traffic signals, we mustn't be stopped."

"You got the law on you?"

"No, but please hurry."

"To where, lady?"

"Here's the address."

"Yes, my cousin said it was Watts. But I can't take you in that roped-off area, you know. I'll drop you as close as I can and you'll have to go on from there on foot."

"Are you sure?"

"Sure am, unless I want some drunk sniper to get me, or some cop, or some trigger-happy Guard. You still want to go? No place for a lady, I can tell you, not tonight."

"Yes, I must go."

There's no help for it. She will walk. She'll make it, too. "Please," she says aloud.

"Okay, it's your funeral," he says, not unkindly.

Is that true? Am I going to die? Why else, all during this past week, has my life seemed to pass in review the way it is said a man drowning sees his entire life flash before him? Shut up, Fiona. Urge this cab onward as fast as it can go because you're on the run now. Face it.

20
Saturday, August 14. 8:00 P.M.

"Can you take the shortest way?" she asks, still whispering.

"I am," he says in a voice far too loud. She is frightened someone may overhear him. "You're on Lincoln, heading for International Airport, and instead of right turn there we go left at Imperial, and that takes you right to Watts. The Santa Monica freeway ain't open yet, or you could of got there quicker."

"How far, then, to Manchester?" she asks through stiff lips, frozen-acting, when really she is burning up with heat. Trickles run down her sides from beneath her arms.

"What's the cross street?"

"I hope to get as near to Eighty-seventh and Figueroa as possible."

"Well, you ain't going to be too bad off because I'll tell you what, I'll take Manchester instead of Imperial."

"Thanks."

"None of my business, but hope you know yours, going into Watts tonight. You better stick to alleys and such."

"I will."

186

The roar of the motor is soothing; he is wasting no time. They must be going fifty miles an hour in a thirty-five-mile zone. Maybe if she distracts him, he will slow down. A ticket, that's all, and the jig will be up, or the nigger will be finished.

"How long have you lived in L.A.?" she asks in a voice quaking out of control.

"I was born here."

"Oh!"

"You born here?"

"No; only been here a few years."

"You got friends in Watts?"

"Yes."

Two little boys, she says to herself, but her chin won't stop quivering. It's only nerves. She can't blame it on rough paving beneath the wheels of the shaking, rushing car because it's smooth now. The driver isn't doing much stopping. He seems to know how to gauge the speed of the taxi to make most of the lights.

"I'll take a hook to the right here, and duck off. I hope to drop you about Western and Manchester, then you got about twelve blocks to Figueroa, and Eighty-seventh only a couple from there. I'll be taking you about seven blocks inside the area if I can get through. They got road blocks everywhere now. I'll tell you it's a hell of a lot quieter tonight then last night, Friday, and it ain't even curfew yet tonight; lacks about half an hour. You got to look sharp. Them cops and Guards are trigger-hungry; they shoot everything that shows. Then you got some snipers too."

"I'll be careful," she says with chin still trembling.

Electric wires reflecting flames from all the fires are colored a deep red. They glow against telephone poles standing

187

out stark, plain and black; sirens wail; snarling trucks dash in all directions. They see the first of the black and white cars. In spite of it all, she must get in there some way; they are her people here who stage this showdown. They won't hurt her. She belongs here. If she ever gets out of her immediate predicament, she'll stay here, somewhere, and live it out with them. So help me, Fiona swears to herself.

The driver makes an unexpected lunging turn of the wheel to the left. "Have to get out of here. Black and whites getting too close up ahead."

Lurching the cab to a staggering stop a block away beneath trees, he cuts the lights and she fumbles a twenty-dollar bill into his hands.

"Good luck," he says, and she knows he hopes she will get out, so he can get himself out of the area before he's in bad trouble.

She gathers the bundle of food, the overnight case, and her purse, and slips out the door to the deserted street. The tail lights of the taxi have already disappeared around the corner. The street is empty. She is alone. It is as though a bomb has been dropped, killing everyone. No lights show in houses or buildings, only naked streetlights and the deep red glowing fingers of searchlights plowing across the sky. They make it too light and bright for cover. She is exposed and now she hears the steady churning roar of a helicopter overhead.

God, it's so damned lonely, so frightening! She wishes the cab at least was still making its noisy turn to streak away. But it's gone; the friendly taxi man is gone. She is alone.

She walks rapidly, keeping on the side street just off Manchester. The sky gleams down on her with a heated, blasting furnace breath; the air is hot and her eyes prickle.

She can feel them itching, but her hands are full and she can't rub them. The farther east she walks, the redder becomes the sky. She clutches the sack of groceries to her left side as though in protection. A fire engine comes down the street with its screaming siren wide open; it deafens her and she shrinks into a doorway and stands there panting. Ahead she spots the first well-manned National Guard road block. There are army jeeps and a deuce-and-a-half truck, as George calls the troop-carrying vehicles. Gathered close are many armed soldiers whose bayonets stick up and glitter on the ends of the long guns they shoulder.

She must turn right and get away from them. If she makes it over another block, she will be closer to Figueroa. She hears no voice shout "STOP!" at her. She hears only sirens whine, and black and white cars roaring by. She begins to skip along faster with little hopping, running steps. Her breath comes in loud gulps, and her heart beats in rapid time against her ribs, while the nightcase bangs against her legs.

"Stop!" She hears the voice this time. Bullets rattle and ping against metal. Someone must be shooting at the fire engine or the black and white cars. Voices scream, "Burn, baby, burn." Others are howling, "Get Whitey."

No, not me, she tells them inside her head. I'm not Whitey. She stumbles off a curb and drops the case; she can't go back for it. It falls open in the gutter and spills out the white blouse. It lies there gleaming while the lights all around are dazzling, and steadily overhead the helicopter roars on and on. All the blend of strident sound encompasses her, and with eyes blinded in the smoke a black face looms close to her. "In here," his voice hisses.

The bullet makes its entry into her leg with a burning,

stinging slap. She shuffles the leg; the groceries crash to the ground and the white curtains spill out as though being displayed deftly for a customer's choice in a shop.

"LOOTER!" she hears. No, no, I am not a looter, she tells them in her head. I am not a looter. I am nothing.

21
Saturday, August 14. 9:00 P.M.

The man yanks her roughly into a gap between two tall buildings; too close to meet the city code, she thinks wildly.

"Follow me. Hang on to my shirt. It's dark here," the voice whispers.

She comes up behind him at the end of the long passage like a rat flushed from its hole into another—a small windowless room where a black shiny young woman says, "Hi," and asks, "You been hurt?"

"I think it's only a nick, my leg," says Fiona.

The black woman, not more than Fiona's own age, bends over her where she sits huddled in a chair.

"I can take care of that. . . . Charley," she says to the man, "get that clean pillow slip in the closet in the other room. It's old, but clean, nice and soft and ready for rags," the woman tells Fiona in soft tones.

Her leg throbs and burns. They think I'm a looter. Out there they shoot, and if they kill you, they claim you resisted them and that's only part of it, because there are hundreds of guns, FBI, National Guard, city, state and county police. George has a gun, so has his wife, and no doubt Humel and his gang, and most of the white citizens, and the agent and the black snipers—so how can I possibly make it to the address? And I must call George someplace and get him here. She feels inside the purse to see if the gun is still there. It is.

"Do you have a telephone?" she asks the woman.

"No." The woman bandages the injured leg.

Fiona sits staring at her upturned hands in her lap. At her wrists, the tiny rhinestones on the cuffs of the raincoat she wears that is crumpled like taffeta are winking and twinkling in the dim light like teardrops; she feels ready to join them in weeping. A tiny glow from a study lamp on a table in the corner does not relieve the gloom. The raincoat nestles down about her with crackling sounds each time she moves away from the gentle ministrations of the woman's hands. It surrounds her body as though alive, lending a feeling of warmth. She eases back against the wall for a moment of repose in the stillness of a cellar room, a bunker in a war.

Her mind won't let her rest. A small radio details on and on in steady voices a running fire of comment on the riot.

How she will like the chance to get on there and tell what she thinks of a society where people are left to become so desperate they resort to the senselessness of all this burning, destroying, and violence! Suddenly the white citizens of Los Angeles are made to realize that all is far from well beneath the carnival-colored lights of this city, where helpless, ignorant blacks are charged more in ghetto stores for their very bread, the same loaf the swells in other areas get for less. Overnight, the black citizens are fed up and filled with the courage for anarchy against the blue-eyed, pale-faced devils who own it all and scheme to keep it from black people. Whitey makes tiny dots by the names of blacks asking for loans to buy car or home. This recording follows a man for the rest of the time he stays here. If he tries to fight through it, he's doomed at the start to failure, beaten by a black spot the size of a pinhead. A black is a risk. Who knows when he can pay?

But somewhere they've got the courage to turn on the lions who've got them cornered. And Whitey is nervous. But Whitey knows he can win in the finish. Protesters can howl until they are hoarse, or even stage a burning, shoot-'em-up party, but they can't win anything. Power is stronger; power fights and beats them back down to where they started, because man is the only animal vile enough to wipe out his own species in war.

The black woman is talking to two male voices in low tones in the other room. Who are they? What do they say about her? The voice on the small radio asks, "What do these Negroes want now?" It answers itself by suggesting, "Let them eat cake someplace, but not in our city. They've got their civil rights." The voice scolds. "Let them get behind their leaders and do something with themselves for them-selves. . . ."

Fiona wants to scream back at the radio voice, "It's an age-old tale, only another slave uprising, a protest against masters." But the man has gone on to political snipers, say-ing the Mayor is taking potshots at the City Council, who all wrangle among themselves over this messy Watts. He says the city police are mad at the Governor, and Fiona feels a weird desire to giggle when the man continues in solemn tones to announce that even professional criminals are hiding out in fear of these intrepid rioters running amok.

The woman comes back and holds a cup of coffee to Fiona's lips. It contains a liberal amount of whiskey. She gulps it down and it burns her throat, but warms her all the way.

The radio voice says a policeman has been shot. The announcer practically shouts the news of this, but then within seconds admits the policeman has been shot by his own nervous, clumsy partner when taking his gun from a police car. Shot in the leg down in Long Beach someplace, where a second uprising is just beginning, the voice suggests more or less happily, and certainly with anticipation if not out and out relish.

"They do exaggerate," the black woman says to Fiona, and she snaps off the radio. "They are repeating over and over a story of a poor black mother and two helpless children being shot by a mean sniper. But later they found it was a personal ruckus of some kind, the woman shot by an ex-boy friend taking advantage of the general atmosphere around here for revenge purposes of some kind."

Fiona says nothing. She thinks of all the fat white mouths going on steadily for some four days now, bad-mouthing blacks every minute of prime time, damning even those guilty of nothing but loss of a job, and not a shop left in the area in which to buy a loaf of bread in case there is any money left to buy it with.

Her headache is a blinding one. The coffee does not help. Her heart pounds, her leg throbs. If only she can sit just one more time in her little house in Venice, about sixteen long miles away from here, turn on the television, and by some good luck see the calming eyes of Martin Luther King as he speaks on a news broadcast, enthralled and taken right out of herself as she listens to his soft, easy, calming voice. She can become so soothed and relaxed she can even contemplate dying with some happiness. All the time she looks and listens to him she has the feeling that a loving hand has been placed in benediction on her head.

It grows late. Better struggle up again and get out to the street. On to Figueroa and find a phone booth and call George on the way. She has a date with him, whether he knows it or not.

"Is there a phone booth near here?" she asks.

"Yes, but it is too risky now. It is after the eight-o'clock curfew. You shouldn't go out now, especially limping."

"There are some groceries out there somewhere on the sidewalk," Fiona says. "Maybe you can use them. Meat and bread and some other things," she adds.

"Oh, go and see quick," the woman says to Charley, and the young man disappears promptly. He returns in minutes with the ragged sack still holding some of the meat and smashed bread.

"That's luck," he says, handing it to the woman.

Fiona sits and her head feels heavy, far too much weight to hold erect. "I must go," she says.

"You may stay here. You shouldn't go out now," the black woman says. "We haven't much to offer you, but there is another room here and you can bunk on the sofa if you like. Tomorrow I think it will be better. My name is Carol Haney and these two young men are my brothers, Carl and Charley. We're the three C's. We've been here

194

about three years now; most of our family is still in Mississippi. We haven't got much, but we've at least got the cockroaches and rats on the run, lots of scrubbing for the bugs and two tough tomcats for the rats. We're saving money for something better than this. We all go to night school. My two brothers car-wash in the daytime—or they did before this thing started—and they go to night school to get their high-school certificates. I do housework and go to UCLA at night. The only reason I'm here at this time of night is that I couldn't make it out of here to get to work this morning. Last night they wouldn't let me out for class; curfew was on and I had to miss. I can get a doctor tomorrow for that leg of yours. I'm studying to become a medical technician and I clean the offices for this doctor on Sundays. I suppose you've had things pretty nice. I guess the way we live here is a kind of shock for you. But you don't need to be afraid here. We three aren't in this thing. It's a problem difficult for outsiders to understand, how so many can exist here without hope, but that makes them do things like this. I mean, transportation is so bad a man can't even get to a job, let alone keep it, and he doesn't have money or credit to buy a decent car. There are no jobs around here. But we're going to have things a lot better later on. Do you work someplace, Miss?"

"No," says Fiona, "not now."

"None of my business, but you're so glamorous and elegant we thought you might have been trying to get to some place of entertainment, an actress or singer or like that. It seemed so important for you to be out tonight."

Carol can be this girl friend Fiona wanted only this morning. Only not any more; it is too late; this morning is too long ago. How old is this black woman? Carol's innocent soft brown eyes look away from her with a shy, evasive glance. She smiles faintly. Does she know what I am?

"I've got more hot coffee in the other room; only take me a minute."

Carol leaves. Fiona has a hard, rocklike something choking her throat closed. Why does she feel like weeping when she looks at ambitious Carol? She is not a weeper, which is most fortunate for the lump. It can move in there and remain. She tries to swallow and gives up. She gets to her feet and winces as her weight falls onto the hurt leg.

"You won't reconsider?" Carol asks, coming in with more coffee.

Fiona opens her handbag to take out the black scarf she's stuffed in there. Careless like, but with craft, she fumbles the roll of money into the scarf. She allows it to fall to her lap when she sits again to put the scarf about her hair. She places it on her head, crosses it beneath her chin, and ties the ends at the back of her neck. Her raincoat is now busy coming to life with many crackings and rustlings because it is hot and dry in Watts, with all the fires blazing and burning it to the ground. She nudges the money roll to the floor, kicking it back with her unharmed leg and sending it beneath her chair.

She stands again. Carol watches. In mind's eye Fiona sees an image of an arrest of a black man at the wheel of his car on the boulevard. "Out, out," barks the black and white; boots smack the pavement and march up to open the black man's car door. The black man is out fast and his stomach is down and he is draped over the hood of his car like a discarded black cleaning rag while the black and

196

white raps him down the back searching in a rat-a-tat-tat beat. The black man arises to get his ticket. When he is lucky, he does, like any man. But mostly he isn't lucky, so he is escorted to the black and white car and his own car is arrested as well and taken away by other cops, even if his wife is sitting in it patiently waiting and saying not a word. However, she is permitted to get out and walk home before the car is impounded and towed away.

Fiona sees this often and in comparison watches the stopping of a Whitey who sits at the wheel of his car, shows driving license to black and white, gets ticket, and drives away.

One time, using the ladies' room at a gas station on the highway at the beach, it is night and the black and whites have a black culprit in chains. The prisoner needs to use the rest room. Fiona is only a nig—they need not temper their ridicule and profane remarks they make to amuse themselves. The prisoner's attempts to relieve himself, restrained by chains on both arms and legs, provide them with endless jollities, all of them obscene.

Watts is Hooverville of Steinbeck's thirties brought up to date, and the Bonus Army at bay in Washington, D. C. It's even American hoods throwing rocks at British soldiers doing guard duty, obeying orders in Boston the cradle of democracy, long ago. When the British soldiers got fed up at being stoned, they opened fire on the rebels and the hoods became the heroes of a new country, but there are no heroes in Watts because they're all criminals. Afterward, when the fires are out, and the law men with guns withdraw, there will be an investigation; the staged inquiry will result in recommendations, one of which will be education for black underdogs and Fiona would suggest the education be given to Whitey in faint hope of changing his attitude toward persons with strange and different-colored skins.

Fiona stands up fine except for wavering, and the raincoat whispers frantic warnings about her. She moves to the door and weaves there and then leans against it to say, "Carol, listen. Whitey is saying, 'Where are your leaders, you Blacks?' He is saying it on television, on the radio, and in the papers. He's crying it huddled terrified at home tonight. 'Where are your leaders?' To help put down this riot, YOU BLACKS STARTED. He does not talk about Our Mutual Leaders—yours, mine, his—a leader of all the people of the country, a leader like the President or even the Governor of the state. No. He shuts us out on the other side, so that's the way Whitey wants it. And that's the way it is. Theirs and ours, separate. Theirs include their hired hands, the black and whites. Charley and Carl ought to be out there right now, getting in their licks, killing black and whites. Do you understand? Instead of 'we shall overcome' by passive resistance, a violent overcoming, futile as that may be, because I know most blacks in Watts have been arrested. Sure, only minor hassling offenses, not even convictions half the time, but that arrest record remains, and there goes a chance at a job. So even up the score; that's all the redress there is. You'll still have this paramilitary force taunting and teasing and daring night and day and arresting, and that is what it's all about, Carol. I mean Whitey's bodyguards, the fuzz, and the palace guards, Whitey's protectors, not mine. Ask a black Guardsman, if you can locate one, and you'll see what's what. Carol, you don't really think that dark skin of yours isn't going to matter?"

198

She sees this strike deep into the flinching eyes of Carol. Now she's got the guts to go into the hail of bullets and general hell on earth waiting outside for her.

"Anything you find around here I left on purpose, a gift from Whitey; not looted, I earned it."

She's out the door and back in the dark passageway, feeling her way along and up through the slit between the buildings. She tips her head in caution around the edge of the bricks. Nothing moves. There must be only a couple of blocks to Figueroa, and then less than one and a half to Eighty-seventh. She can make it—because she has to. There is nothing else for her anywhere.

22
Saturday, August 14. 10:00 P.M.

Fiona sees the large dead dog strung up high on wires at the top of a telephone pole. "Hang by the neck until dead" flashes across her mind. She hears birds, huddled in clusters in tops of trees along the curb, cheetering and cheering themselves up amid chaos. In a window box attached to a building she passes a sign that reads "Beauty Parlor," and there is a drift of scarlet flowers. The panes of glass are scrawled with "Owned by a blood brother," and the glass is not broken. She pauses to bend over the flowers to catch the perfume, but there is only the strong stink of burning rubber, hot tar, brick dust, and cordite to be scented anywhere tonight, even in flowers.

She steps along past charred and smoking buildings and soon comes to an area where fires rage, crack, snap, and spew forth billows of smoke. They are way out of control and her every breath is one of choking in a stench of molotov cocktails and the acrid odor of spilled whiskey trickling over the broken glass of the sidewalk.

Beside her, for only a moment, walks another sign of life, a skinny, toeing-in cat, that furtively sniffs and then darts up another alley. Fiona enters it too.

The cat stops to lurk by a fence until she gets by. In the backyards she can see padlocks and chains on shed doors, gates, and garages, even on back doors. And cans are chained to white picket fences.

Even here glass slithers and grates beneath her tread. She steps around gleaming wet smears that can be anything—blood, booze, or only muddy water. A new sofa, of the make, color, and price to attract and bilk the poor, sits unaccountably across the end of the alley. It is brilliant turquoise and marked in plaids of silver, gold, and copper threads already tarnished. Its stiff wooden legs gleam with cheap varnish. Perhaps the manufacturers hope it gets home and sat on once or twice before the legs break.

Light poles on the next street ahead are twisted into odd shapes and lean in drunken attitudes; sheets of glass are broken out in jagged shards from shop windows. New, obscenely white bed sheets, shiny pots and pans glitter where they've been dropped along the gutter. Tipped-over cars, some with wheels still slowly revolving, line the middle of the street.

Fiona stumbles over a cluster of spent bullets and thinks about the fact she's now an ordinary black girl in an extraordinary situation. A battlefield. In Venice, in a snug cement house covered in ivy, she is a strange exotic character stuck into a most ordinary background. She never matches anywhere. What an odd thing that now she is shut into this setting with no way out, all exits blocked. She is suddenly a prisoner. There are only false exits from Watts, the black ghetto. An armed insurrection is in progress and only enemy troops are permitted inside to put it down. They come equipped for the job, and will waste no time polishing off this ragged inept rebellion.

All ordinary things look strange. Unlighted gasoline stations, with all their beckoning advertising gimmicks, are dark and stilled; only tiny colorful flags still flutter. The cafés and shops are blank, deserted, locked or broken into. Rubble is strewn in the streets, and the sidewalks are difficult to walk on. The mysterious air of the city, smelling of gunpowder and shot, matches Fiona's mood. She wishes she could be a soldier in an army, say Israel, where a woman wears a uniform and carries a gun and fights the enemy.

She crunches along, wondering where the enemy is hiding. Grit crackles beneath her tread and sometimes she trips over a board. Brick and glass lean crazily out from bent frames, so she must walk through it all or go around it. Her mouth and nose are scorched by the stinging smoke of all the fires. Most of Los Angeles appears to be burning down. It must be so, for, from inside the ring of fire looking out, there cannot be a place left where fires are not out of control.

Within herself, she feels a matching fire, a desire to take

action with George, the main target, destroy him, and live in peace. She can't turn back now because she is too eager for war, just as keen as George for war.

With her head down and minding her step, with the limping leg beginning to send signals of pain up and down, she picks her way along steadily, getting closer by the minute to Eighty-seventh Street at last. She looks up too late.

"Hiya baby," screams a voice in her ear, so close she can smell the whiskey-laden frantic breath. "Y'all ought to get to hell outta here, baby. Ain't safe for a fat persian from Beverly Hills. We overcome tonight, baby; freedom now, baby. Old Whitey sharing blood tonight," the man says, walking close to her, dogging her. "That's what bugs 'em, baby, that blood-sharing. Get with us or get beat up, baby. How come you don't listen, baby? You been sharing with honkey over there?" and he holds her arms in a pinching grasp.

"I live just over there," she says, and a group gathers solidly about them in seconds.

Just ahead she sees the sign in the middle of the street:

TURN LEFT OR BE KILLED

A howl of happiness goes up from the crowd about her, and a boy yells in feverish excitement, "Hey, here come the sons of bitches. Let's get the mother fuckers, come on!"

Fiona is swooped forward on the run. If only she can find George, she whimpers to herself with spent breath, gulping for air and trying not to cry. But she hasn't called him. There aren't any phones in the alleys she's been walking. She hasn't made it to the boys' house either. If only she can, then maybe the agent will help her. He wants her alive. Maybe even Humel will help.

Now the black-and-whites are organized. They string themselves across the street, twenty abreast in solid row of black and white. They carry guns at the ready for attack, they move forward in a springy crouch, and now there are olive-drab Guardsmen among them too. They come ever closer and without a break in the line, like the Redcoats in the Revolutionary War. No breakthrough in that line anywhere for poor Fiona.

But there—oh, my God, there—thank God, there's George in a jeep, standing tall up there beside the driver.

"George, it's me," she screams.

All the black faces turn on her; streaked in sinister soot and the dust of battle, they turn as one to look at her. "Who in Christ do y'all know up there?" they howl at her.

"No one there," she lies, shaking her head vigorously. And so intent are they on the coming clash, they ignore her to press on. She's insane to cry to George for help. He wants her in this position. She can't learn her lesson that she's nothing but a threat and has been all her life. She's a superfluous birth, a material thing, a commodity bought and sold. She will never command even a steadfast companion, much less a ring. George is deploying troops to win an advance and she's expendable, just as she has been all her life.

Oh, she must make George see her. She stares at his face. It is on fire with elation. He shouts, "Get ready to let 'em have it. Over their heads first, men. . . . They're not turning left. . . . Fire," he screams.

She starts to run. "Get that jigaboo; she's turning right," shouts a cop. Only to get to George, she tells him inside her head.

A rock whistles by her arm. Its jagged edge tears the

raincoat. She looks down at it as jostling bodies stream by her and help to tear it into two strips down her back. Its shredded sides cling along her arms like twin chiffon draperies. It sags down her leg, the hurt one that throbs as though set on fire too. The pant's leg is torn. . . . Oh, God, let her get George's attention.

She waves her arms draped in ragged raincoat like a scarecrow in a field, but elated George is more than half blind with pride in his splendid assignment. Right now he's directing the charge to knock over this lousy army—poorly uniformed, poorly organized, poorly equipped, lousy civilian rabble. Let them play soldier; let them get to hell in uniform properly then; learn to kill the right way.

Fiona knows this is what he is thinking; she knows him well.

She pants against a building, staring at George the humanist, the Middle Ages man, the big bull colonel in his element. She gasps for breath against the cracked building. Its door hangs askew and its bricks spill down its sides in heaps on the sidewalk. Yes, George will go to heaven. He has lived right, even suffered, stuck in the lousy National Guard when born to be a regular Daniel; a good math man, too, a wife, and a couple of kids to carry on, even a mistress to take up the slack, and lots of that, and he's white like angels. The devil is black, always black; black for death and white for life. How will it be with blacks at the top? No one knows. It can't happen. Light at the top is a law of some kind; black at the bottom. It is better balance in art, better fashion in costume, everyone in the world can be eventually assimilated into the mass—Jews, wops, micks, everyone, as long as the skin is light. But not blacks; never blacks; too dark for breeding. I'll take some light meat, please; white meat, please, no dark for me, thanks just the same.

Fiona is buffeted out of her doorway and, along with the mob, caught fast in the forward surge. There is no law of the land, only war between haves and have-nots. Fiona is with the have-nots. George may be decorated for his part in this, putting down these huddled, yearning masses burning for redress. A sudden roaring motor deafens Fiona and she trips over the sagging raincoat that grips her advance like leg irons.

She falls. A trickle of brilliant, bright-red blood, unbelievably bright, crawls in a lazy descending line from her hair, swings out from her forehead, and hangs in a narrow silk thread before her eyes.

She forces herself to her feet, tearing at the raincoat that binds her. She dashes forward again, limping, hopping, and scrabbling along the block. She stops to fumble at the solidness of the long wall of closed-tight windows and doors, seeking an opening anywhere along its length, tearing her hands, clawing the brick. There is no opening.

Bullets spatter about her and into her and she slides down the solid wall like a forgotten bundle of overdried clothes at the washhouse. She rests in a huddled clump on the sidewalk. The picture on the dead dark television screen appears in a fine haze before her. With eyes wide open, she looks again at the leafy trees, the nodding flowers, and she hears a low singing in her ears—peace. . . .

The shiny black boot nudges at the shiny-black-raincoat-draped body. It responds with a faint whisper and a sigh and a stirring. Fiona feels nothing—not even solid black boots—even though her eyes are wide open. . . . She is dead.